To Dennis,
Thank you for b
never gives up.

Angel School

MY ANGEL

Richard Sweatman

Contents

	V
Prologue	1
1. Chapter 1	3
2. Chapter 2	11
3. Chapter 3	19
4. Chapter 4	25
5. Chapter 5	32
6. Chapter 6	47
7. Chapter 7	59
8. Chapter 8	76
9. Chapter 9	87
10. Chapter 10	98
11. Chapter 11	106
12. Chapter 12	117
13. Chapter 13	125
14. Chapter 14	132
15. Chapter 15	139

> # 16. Chapter 16

Copyright ©2024 by Richard Sweatman

All rights reserved.

No part of this publication may be reproduced, distributed, or transmitted in any form or by any means, including photocopying, recording, or other electronic or mechanical methods, without the prior written permission of the publisher, except as permitted by U.S. copyright law. For permission requests, contact: richard.sweatman29@gmail.com

The story, all names, characters, and incidents portrayed in this production are fictitious. No identification with actual persons (living or deceased), places, buildings, and products is intended or should be inferred.

ISBN 13: 979-8-3003-8138-7

First edition 2024

Prologue

Before anything existed, God looked at everything He had made. Among all the stars and planets, Earth was special to Him because that's where His human children would live. God knew that humans would need help finding their way back to Him, so He decided to create special helpers - guardian angels.

In Heaven, a place filled with amazing light and colors, God began creating these angels. Each one was different and special, made from God's own light and love. They had one main job: to help and protect humans during their life on Earth.

This is the story of one of these guardian angels named Shiloh. God held Shiloh in His hands and breathed life into him, teaching him everything he would need to know. Like a parent giving their child special gifts, God gave Shiloh powers and abilities that would help him do his job.

Shiloh was special. God gave him the ability to really understand how humans feel, and a strong desire to help them. As God sang a beautiful song over Shiloh, his future began to take shape.

There's a battle happening that most humans can't see - a fight between good and evil, between light and darkness. Shiloh would be part of this battle, helping to protect humans and guide them back to God. His adventures would take him from the beautiful courts of Heaven to Earth, showing how God's love works in ways we can't always see.

This is Shiloh's story - about how guardian angels learn to help humans, how they fight against evil spirits, and how they work with God's plan. Through Shiloh's eyes, we'll see how Heaven and Earth are connected, and how guardian angels work hard to protect people.

You see, every person has guardian angels watching over them. We can't see them, but they're always there, helping us fight against evil and darkness. They do this because God loves us and wants to keep us safe.

Now, let's begin our story in Heaven, where Shiloh opens his eyes for the first time, ready to start his journey as a guardian angel...

Chapter 1

Origins of a Guardian Angel

"Shiloh!"

"Shiloh, where are you?" said a distant voice. The voice had the appearance to be coming from deep down, somewhere.

"Shiloh!"

I realised that this was my Father's voice that thundered through the infinite expanse of Heaven, shaking me from my peaceful slumber. I stirred within the cradle of His mighty palm, opening my eyes to gaze upwards at His brilliance.

Prismatic light radiated from Him, dancing across my form in kaleidoscopic hues. The raw power contained within each syllable He spoke resonated through every fibre of my being. I blinked, squinting against the dazzling display surrounding me.

"Yes, Father?" I answered, my voice but a whisper compared to His cosmic roar.

"Hey, Shiloh, you are next," said my Dad as he lifted me high up and cradled me in his large hands.

The memory of those words 'You are next', filled me with a sense of destiny. I remember that wonderful voice, the voice of my Dad. Yes, He spoke all those years ago when I was just a thought.

I am an angel, not just any angel, but a special type: I am a guardian angel.

My first visual memory of my Dad is me in the palm of his hand, feeling warm and bathed in wonderful colours and light that flowed right through me. I remember squinting into the light and, as the waves came over me, I gained a glimpse of His fiery blue eyes. They were blue and, as I looked, I flowed back into Him again. The connection between us was tangible. I was part of Him, yet simultaneously able to be separate in space.

And His voice, full of life, created whatever He spoke. It rolled over me like a storm, impregnating me with thoughts and ideas and filling my mind with pictures and scenes that only He knew about. Yet they seemed to be all there for me to discover and experience. He was speaking my destiny into me.

The words from His mouth flowed over me and encircled me, and then became part of me. I was morphing into the words: we became one. I remember His words were loaded with love, and it was a wonderful feeling.

I recall Him saying, "Shiloh, your name is Shiloh. I'm going to send you to another place, where you will take great care of My children. You will protect and help them in their quest to find Me. You will do great and mighty deeds. I have placed in you many talents and We will teach you many new things. You will always be with Me, and you will do My bidding."

Then He put me back inside Himself and I travelled deep inside Him, where the others slept. A happy feeling enveloped me, and I dreamed of all the special things I would do.

Time passed, though I must add that it does not have any hold on us in the heavenly Kingdom. There, we were free from the constraints time had on Earth, the home of my Father's children.

Sometimes, I would awaken and feel giggly, laughter flow out of me.

My Father loved to tickle me, and I would stretch myself out as He blew His breath over me. It danced across my body and contained many thousands of laughing tickles.

He loved to watch my face light up and often would throw a large booming rumble of laughter from deep down inside of Him, and it would roll out and resonate deep down inside me.

It shook everything and filled the air with a sweet fragrance and, as the laugh landed on me, it seemed to engulf and twist me around and upside down and go right through me, all at the same time.

The colours of His song for me – yes, my own song from Him – were enchanting.

My precious child, your time has come,

To leave your home, your journey's begun.

I made you for a purpose true,

A mighty task I have for you.

I call you now, go forth,

CHAPTER 1

Protect my children, those of earth.
Though darkness falls, your light will shine,
My strength and love will be your guide.
Shiloh, Shiloh, you'll never walk alone,
Shiloh, Shiloh, I'm with you as you roam.
Shiloh, Shiloh, you have my heart and soul,
Shiloh, Shiloh, we'll reach our destined goal.
The path ahead will challenge you,
But I have equipped you, this is true.
Stay near to me, obey my voice,
And lead my children, help them make their choice.
Shiloh, Shiloh, you'll never walk alone,
Shiloh, Shiloh, I'm with you as you roam.
Shiloh, Shiloh, you have my heart and mind,
Shiloh, Shiloh, we'll reach our destined goal.
I made you with my own great love,
Sent from my kingdom high above,
I call you forth, go and be the mighty guardian.
Yes, you are my brave guardian angel.

The words danced around me and landed on my skin. I was an apprentice. As my Dad sang over me, I floated up and out of the safety of His hand. I felt brave and knew somehow, deep down, that this separation from the depth within my Dad was good. I felt excited and floated further away.

I remember glancing around. Now, for the first time, I observed my entire Dad. He was all flashing lights and swirling colours and brightness, even within dark clouds, but I could just about make out His shape sitting on a large throne. He looked like me! He had a body like mine, but bigger, and I have no flashing lights swirling with stormy clouds and a thundering voice. But hey, I am working on that.

Someone called me. He wore a bright, white, shimmering cloak, tied with a broad golden belt with a large buckle, and a royal purple sash was slung over his right shoulder, falling across his chest to his left hip. On his feet, he had strapped sandals.

Please understand that I did not know what any of these were or even why they were worn. All I had on my own body was a linen cloak, my toes were uncovered, and I had no belt or fancy sash. My cloak did not even shimmer, it was just clean, white, and new, but I could still feel my Dad in it and smell that exceptional fragrance.

The shimmering, sashed being said again, "Come down here, Shiloh."

How? I can remember wondering how to get down there. I was still drifting on my Dad's voice. It pulsated and engulfed me. I looked at the figure below, grinning back at me. All around him were other ones like me. They were standing on green grass that was waving from side to side and calling out to me, softer and squeakier, sounding like millions of whispers.

The others standing around the sashed being all joined in. Everyone was yelling with excitement, giving many directions.

"Look where you want to go, then desire it. Come on, it's easy!"

"Just throw yourself into it!" came another voice.

Then one of them, on the command of the shiny guy, came up to me. He just lifted himself up and, what I know now is: he flew to me. A board of light supported him as he travelled at lightning speed to me.

"Hi, I'm Seymour," he said with a broad grin. He held out his hand, and we touched. As we did, many thoughts flashed before me, flooding my deep self with images and sounds like I had never heard or seen before. They were different to my Dad's thoughts.

"Wow, what was that?"

"That is me. These are all the things I have learned and seen and now you have them too."

"But that is so weird. It is strange to me!"

"Yip, but within is the instruction on how to ride the beam."

"Ride the beam? Oh, that board of light! OK yes, I get it!"

As I imagined the beam, it was there. It paused in front of me and hummed. I climbed onto it and Seymour shot off ahead, calling out, "Yahoo!"

He swooped down and landed next to the group.

My turn – "Yahoo!" I called out, but nothing … well, not nothing. I could hear the group laughing, but also encouraging me again.

Next to me was a huge angel. He had a fiery sword and wings on his back. His cloak blazed with waves of fire. On his wrist was a band of strange emblems and writing, which changed every now and again. His eyes reminded me of my Father's but lacked His intense love. It was like a lesser version, but more ferocious, not so kind and loving.

"What's your name, boy?"

CHAPTER 1

"Shiloh," I replied.

"Well, Master Shiloh, are you going to float here all day and let your classmates out-do you, or are you going to ride that board?"

He had a sneaky grin on his smooth, shimmering face, and I glimpsed friendliness.

"Feel the board, boy, then think about where you want to go. We will meet again, Master Shiloh," he added, "I look forward to working with you. Now ride that board and remember, you are a mighty angel and master of the board."

It felt as if he was calling out a memory from deep within me, from among those that Seymour had just deposited.

I looked down at the group – my 'classmates' – who were waiting with bated breath. The board moved slowly forward, but not as fast and swanky as it had been with Seymour. However, I was able to glide down and even had time to glance around.

The large angel that had been chatting to me was cruising together with a hundred or more others, who were swooping and diving in perfect formation, synchronising with each other in one unified group. I approached on the board and stopped next to my classmates.

"Who was that?" I asked one of them.

"That, young Shiloh, was Michael. He is an archangel and is the commander of the army."

"What did he say to you up there?" asked another classmate, almost bursting with excitement.

"OK, that's enough now, class," an angel, who felt older than the rest of us, said. Shiloh, you are the last member of class 84, welcome to Angel School." I realised that the angel was my new teacher and mentor Ralph. He gazed at me kindly, his brown eyes crinkling at the corners. "Welcome Shiloh. We have been expecting you."

I looked around at the other young angels surrounding me. Their faces shone with excitement and curiosity.

Ralph rested a hand on my shoulder. "Come, let me show you around your new home."

We walked across a shimmering pearl courtyard, my feet barely touching the smooth surface. All around us spread a vision of paradise. Lush gardens bloomed, overflowing with exotic plants and flowers from across the cosmos. Their perfumes intermingled, creating a symphony of sweet scents.

Delicate butterflies with rainbow wings fluttered from flower to flower, their jewel-toned bodies glinting in the soft light. Strange new fruits hung heavy on the branches, their skins a mosaic of vivid colours I had no name for yet.

How I knew then what all these flowers and stuff were – well, it all came from the deposit of my Father, and the added download from Seymour.

As I looked at things, I would get an inkling of what it was and if it intrigued me, I was made aware of all the details I needed to understand the object, its purpose, form, everything.

One fruit captured my attention, large and teardrop-shaped, carved from purple crystal, veined with gold. As I gazed at it, knowledge awoke within me – plumella, the celestial fruit. Taking one bite would impart days' worth of nourishment. Not that we would need the food value, but I just knew it would taste amazing. Strange, all these new senses, and my adventure was just beginning.

Ralph smiled at my awestruck expression. "Here in the gardens of the Most High, you will find wonders beyond imagination. And this is only the beginning."

I tore my eyes from the garden as we approached a towering waterfall, liquid diamonds cascading down sheer cliffs. At the base lay an inviting pool, the waters a clear turquoise that sparkled, as if lit from within.

"This will be our outdoor classroom," Ralph said, gesturing around us. "Here you will learn many lessons about using your angelic abilities to serve our Father."

I could not contain my excitement. For as long as I could remember, I had longed for this moment. Although I had just been released from my Fathers presence, the Father had installed a deep desire for me to serve the Kingdom. I wanted nothing more than to understand my purpose and use the gifts my Father had bestowed upon me.

As if reading my mind, Ralph smiled. "I know you are eager and curious, young one. Together we will nurture your talents. But angelhood comes with grave responsibility. You must commit to these studies."

I nodded. "I understand. And I am ready."

Ralph squeezed my shoulder before continuing the tour. As he gazed down at me, his ancient eyes filled with wisdom. I nodded, my heart pounding with anticipation.

Ralph turned and swept his arm in an arc. "This is the Realm of Light, where young angels master skills to serve the Kingdom."

As I followed his gesture, the scenery came alive in my senses. The azure sky shone like an endless crystalline sea, so clear that I could notice galaxies swirling in its depths. Lush

CHAPTER 1

meadows rolled over gentle hills, dotted with exotic flowers in every colour of the rainbow. Their sweet fragrance perfumed the air. Trees with silver leaves chimed in the soft breeze, creating an ethereal melody.

We walked along a path bordered by trees with silver leaves that harmonised like bells in the breeze. Angels flitted by on shimmering wings, smiling in greeting. The crystal towers of a palace glimmered ahead, with tall spires that pierced the sapphire sky.

"That is the Great Hall where we take our lessons," Ralph said, pointing to the largest crystal structure. "And over there is the Room of Contemplation, where you can commune with the Father."

My eyes widened, trying to take it all in. Everything glowed with an inner light, dazzling to behold.

As we entered the Great Hall, I gasped. The soaring, arched ceiling depicted scenes of angels at work across the cosmos. Rows of consoles faced a raised dais where Ralph would teach. Other young angels murmured, waving me over.

"Welcome, brother!" said one with a shock of dark curls, adding, "We are eager to begin our training together with you."

I gazed at their smiling faces and felt a sense of belonging. Each one emanated an inner light, though not as bright as my Father's. Their grace and poise marked them as celestial beings.

Now Ralph addressed us as one. "Here at the Academy," he said, "you will prepare for your duties as guardian angels. Lessons will cover everything from manifesting your wings to guiding human souls."

A thrill rushed through me. Guide human souls! I could hardly wait to meet one. What would they be like?

As if reading my mind, Ralph chuckled and directed his gaze to me. "Patience, young one. You must start with the basics. First, you must learn to master your wings. Manifest them," I closed my eyes, sensing energy swirling within me. Focusing, I willed my wings into being. A collective gasp made me open my eyes.

To my surprise, iridescent wings had unfurled from my back, glimmering like mother of pearl. I fluttered them, delighting in the sensation.

Ralph led us to the edge of the courtyard which dropped away into an endless azure sky.

"Now, one by one, allow the joy of flight to lift you!"

My friend Seymour went first, his downy wings beating faster until he lifted off the ground. He swooped and dove, performing twists and loops. His laughter rang out. The others followed, zipping through the heavens.

Soon it was my turn. I stepped to the edge, gazing down at the expanse below. I felt a touch of fear, but also exhilaration.

Taking a deep breath, I ran and leapt into the open air. For a heart-stopping moment I plunged downwards. Then my wings caught the updraft, and I soared upwards, the wind rushing against my face. It was beyond anything I could ever know or imagine. I knew I was going to enjoy this training and what adventures lay ahead.

"Well done, Shiloh! Now, all of you, come back and we will take a closer look at the citadel, the Great Hall. Ralph turned and swept his arm in an expansive gesture. "Here is the Citadel of Light, where guardian angels like yourself master their abilities before being assigned to the mortal realm."

I gazed in awe at the soaring spires of the citadel, built from a crystalline material that caught the light and fractured it into a thousand rainbow hues. The windows blazed as if giant diamonds were embedded within the walls. It was more stunning than anything I had ever seen.

Ralph led me back through arched hallways lined with statues of venerable angels. Their stone eyes followed us as we passed. Other young angels fluttered by, chatting as they headed to their classes. The halls rang with joyful laughter and snatches of heavenly music.

We re-entered the Great Hall, and I noticed that the vaulted ceilings, painted with scenes I now saw included angels helping lost souls. Ralph returned to take his place at the dais.

"This is where you will learn the history of our realm and the mortal worlds," he said. "Study hard, pay attention, and you will be prepared for your sacred duties."

"Here you will learn to manifest all your abilities," Ralph said. "You must hone your energy into light to create objects, understand divine laws to bend time and space, and focus your intent to transport yourself instantly."

I couldn't wait for my education to begin!

Chapter 2

Celestial Classroom

The Great Hall's vast courtyard had massive pillars that had writing on all sides, but even as I watched, the writing changed into moving pictures. The floor of the classroom was made of clear crystal that lit up now and again with images of many wonderful things, which sprang into life.

I learned later there are similar objects on earth, which are called flat TV screens that can be viewed in 3D. Man would sit in front of these for hours.

The earthly things there, even the advanced holograms, are just a mere glimpse, a passing shadow of what I could see into and experience in heaven. Sometimes the images would manifest from out of the screens and the teacher would give us a lesson on what they were about.

We were told to sit on seats, which were like small thrones. They had a comfy feeling, for, as I sat down, the chair cuddled up around me, and we fitted together snugly. Everything in heaven was so alive!

Ralph, stood up in front of the class and addressed us pupils.

"As your teacher, my job is to get you ready for your tasks that lie ahead. You have an important job that I will tell about in due course.

First, you must learn as much as you can about the Kingdom of God, which is here, and is your home."

Then, waving his arm, he gestured to all that we could observe from our level in the classroom, and far out, back to where I had travelled from. Now I knew that there were many levels in heaven and the throne room was elevated, exalted above everything else. It was the heaven of heavens.

The sounds emanating from it were still rumbling across the sky and flashes of light mixed with the intense, bright colours. The light and sounds were all alive here, pulsating and changing and ever increasing. They flooded us with warm feelings of pure, rich love. Yes, even we angels need to feel loved.

The sky was filled with many other beings. Some were like me and had just a pair of retractable wings, and they glided about . But all were busy doing something, carrying stuff, or collecting stuff. Some held scrolls, carrying messages, others had great weaponry and were mighty warriors indeed!

The classroom now forgotten, I glanced again towards the throne and now could noticed other mighty, living creatures.

Some had six wings and flew around the throne. They bowed down and covered their faces and their feet, calling out, "Holy! Holy is the Lord! Holy, Holy, Holy, Lord God Almighty! Who was and is and is to come!" Each time they proclaimed this, it filled the atmosphere with great pleasure and intense love coming from the One on the throne. The pleasure and love were mixed with outstanding authority and power, which streamed forth.

As I observed, an urge from deep within overtook me and I also bowed down, submitting to this kingly Creator, who sat in unapproachable Light, aware that everything in heaven and earth was made for Him and through Him and to Him! Praise erupted from me to Him as I joined many thousands upon thousands of angels, ten thousand times ten thousand! The throne vibrated, releasing an array of vibrant, living rainbow colours, mixed with lightning and smoke and booming thunder that sounded like many voices!

The waves of His power and presence rolled over me, into me and all around me with palpable intensity, until I found myself back in the classroom. It was magnificent. The pillars stretched up so high you could not tell where they ended, and they were made of moving, living light. Like the crystal floor, the images that flowed from them and through them I did not yet understand. This was my classroom!

Heaven is a place of such large possibilities, even we angels only know a fraction of what is, and the Father is always busy with the secret mission. None of us yet knows what it is, only the Father and His Son Jesus and the Holy One know. We in the classroom sensed they were getting excited, and we expected them to say something soon.

Our teacher spoke.

CHAPTER 2

"You will meet Jesus and the Holy One, and that will be your best day yet. Jesus is like your Father. He and the Holy One are intertwined together, all together as One, but they have different jobs. There are rumours of the secrets about to be told, and the Father wants you to be part of it – you need to be ready.

We have much to teach you. Just as Michael has his job, which is important, the Father says that your job will be just as important."

All the time, Ralph was looking into our eyes and watching every reaction in us. Nothing could be hidden or go unnoticed. He grinned and added, "This is going to be fun and purposeful. You were created for a time like this, and only you can do this significant task.

"Now, Seymour, as you think you are the best, maybe you can instruct the rest of us about how we become invisible," he said, with a sneaky grin.

I wondered what the word even meant. Then, Seymour disappeared. He was there right in front of us, and in the next instant was gone! As I looked around the room, I felt the warm breath and heard the giggle of Seymour.

"Wow, it is you," I said, as I touched and felt his face. He had long white hair that was braided in tight rows. I ran my hand over them.

"It is you!" I said.

Then, there he was again, visible and grinning, right next to me.

"Seymour, would you like to show the class how you managed that task?"

"Well, all you do is concentrate on your surroundings and bring them forward over you. That way, what was behind you is now in front, and as you move forward, you just keep imagining the scenery changes, and it adapts to where you are. If you can project the scene from behind you to the front, then you will be invisible," said Seymour, looking around to check if anyone else had vanished.

I was checking my surroundings and imagined them to be in front of me, when Seymour laughed.

"Well, Shiloh, not bad."

I was invisible! It worked! I could see and reached forward to tickle Seymour when I reappeared and became visible again.

"Ah, you need to constantly be projecting your surroundings, Master Shiloh, don't forget, or you will be visible again. But well done, few pupils get it so quickly," said the teacher.

This is great, I thought. I can get away and explore and nobody will even know I am there. My mind wondered about all the amazing places I could go to explore, when a voice in my head said, "But Shiloh, I will know and will keep a keen eye on you."

The teacher said this with a grin, but I looked, and his mouth was closed the whole time! He continued, "Yes, Master Shiloh, I can read all your minds at will and even put thoughts into yours. Be patient, you have much to learn."

I noticed he was pleased with me, even though I had been distracted by personal plans.

Seymour smiled. "Yes, I can even intercept thoughts and replace them. Cool, hey."

We were all summoned to the front of the quad. As I walked over the crystal squares, they lit up with bright colours and pictures. We got to the edge, and there was a great big hole going down into a vortex of mist.

"This is a portal to earth. There we will observe many wonderful things. Today we are going to a part of the kingdom where we will interact with other beings. They are known as animals," said the teacher.

Hodge, who was also a young one, asked, "What is an animal?"

"Ah, animals are part of the great secret that the Father and Son are busy with. Jesus told me a while ago that they will be crucial to the success of the future. So, our job now is to learn all about them and know how to have a good relationship with them and even use them to our advantage," said Ralph, while looking into my eyes.

As he spoke, I saw a flash of brown and white break through the mist. Loud, shrill waves of sound came up and over us. They were of purple and green colours, swirling around and making shapes across the sky.

The teacher said, "Does anyone know what that is saying?"

Hodge screamed out, "Jump!"

"Yes, Hodge, well done. Those shapes are all important for you to learn. Remember them, as they will one day help you," said Ralph.

"Well, what are you waiting for?" yelled Seymour, as he leapt over the edge and disappeared into the swirling mist below. Only the sound of his excited laughter could be heard.

I looked at the teacher, who just stood, with his right eyebrow twitching.

We all plummeted down into the mist after I jumped over the edge.

I was not screaming with excitement, though, and my whole body was stiff and, just as I was wondering 'what now?' – there it was, swooping into my flight path – a gigantic creature with a broad back and feathers. It rose under me, and I settled upon its back.

CHAPTER 2

I had seen something similar before. Yes! The wings on Michael's back! Was this Michael's army? I thought.

"No, Master Shiloh," Ralph intercepted my thoughts. "These creatures are called eagles. They are fierce hunters and eat only meat. They have a keen eye and will see what you cannot see." I looked at him in confused wonder. "Never mind, Shiloh. For now, all you need to do is enjoy the ride."

I held on tight with one hand and with the other stroked the soft covering of its back as we swooped down through the clouds into a wonderful open place.

The colour green was everywhere, moving, flowing, and singing. Yes, all praising my Dad. I puffed out my chest and joined in, we all did, laughing and tumbling around in the air, falling off and being caught again and even being flung from one eagle to another as they somersaulted.

It was so much fun! We stayed in the air for a long time. The teacher explained how we could direct the eagles left or right. These were yet further new concepts, which, however, I inexplicably understood straight away.

As I thought, "Go left," the eagle dipped his huge wings, and we banked away to the left, and there, suspended in front of us, was a large rock with a hole the size of the eagle's wingspan. "Let's go through that!"

The eagle, for the first time, turned his head and said, "Are you sure, kid?"

"Yes, go! Let's do it!"

With a twinkle in his clear blue eyes, he said, "Well, young Shiloh, hang on!"

The eagle tucked his wings in, and we exploded in speed towards the rock. The air was whistling past us so quickly as we approached, that the praises of the green trees and fields were muffled. Then we were through the hole in the rock! The eagle rolled several times in a victory salute. All I could do was hold on, before yelling with all my might, "Hal-le-lu-yah!"

"Ha ha," laughed the eagle, "You have just completed the last part of this course. I think we should not get too far ahead." The grin on his face was ever so slight, but I noticed his eyes were now orange coloured. The change in realms had transformed him. His eyes sparkled.

"We had best join the others then," I said.

"Yes, but Shiloh, you and I will have much fun together again soon," he replied.

We landed on a cliff face, still hundreds of meters above the ground, which was green and brown and moving constantly. Sounds of singing flowed up to us in waves of orange, yellow and green light. The harmonious sounds were praising my Dad. The waves became rays of many colours, flashing and intertwining, spiralling upwards before shooting off towards the portal. There were other angels much larger than us, who had sparkling, golden-lined gowns, and they were catching the waves of these songs and putting them into large barrels.

I asked the teacher why they did that. He smiled and said, "Because the Father lets no praise from His creation slip by Him unnoticed. He delights in all He has made. Even the trees that clap their hands and the mountains and hills, which break out in shouts of joy before Him."

As the whole of the class stood on the ledge, Ralph said, "How many other animals can you observe? Look carefully, and then look again, deeper."

I looked and could see small shapes moving in the green background, but that was it. Then the teacher said, "Look again."

This was the key. Seymour was grinning, leaning back on the rock face.

He said, "Look again and again."

So, I focused on the grey shape and intensified my stare, again and again. Wow! As I did this, I got closer and closer. , I grabbed hold of the angel nearest to me, whose name was Jasper. He looked at me and asked,

"You OK?"

"Ah, yes, I think so, Jasper! I thought I was there with that animal! He was so big and was rumbling. He had an long nose that he was grabbing grass with and putting into his mouth."

"You were right here with us, you never left," replied Jasper, gesturing and pointing to the spot I was standing on.

"Shiloh, you are a quick learner for sure, but you must not get ahead of yourself," the teacher said, grinning at Seymour. "Actually communing with the animal is for another lesson," he said. "Right now, I want you to practice spotting the animals in the grass and count how many types you see. Remember, there are small and big, long and short shapes, all sizes and all manner of things."

I stood, looking again, fixing my gaze at the waving grass. The waves of colour flowed with such elegance it was distracting, but I concentrated on the lighter-coloured creature. Again, I was right up close to it, I just couldn't help it. He had dark eyes and golden yellow surrounding the dark black pupils. He blinked into the light. His nose was moving from side to side.

CHAPTER 2

Then his mouth opened and widened, displaying glistening white teeth, long white teeth, and a pinkish red tongue, like mine, but exceptionally long! He was yawning. He shook his colossal head and the fur, long and dark around his head and shoulders, moved from side to side in a swishing motion.

From his side emerged a much smaller version of him, which jumped up onto his neck, dangled from his paws, and then they both rolled onto the ground. The little one stood tall and strong over his dad in a mock warrior poise, and his dad just watched.

Then, with ease, the little one was flipped off onto the ground. They were part of a group, and the other ones were all lying on the grass under an enormous umbrella tree, which had long thorns and clusters of yellow flowers. I heard Ralph instruct us to look closer.

As I did, I could see tiny wings moving. They moved so fast that the air whirled around them, and a sharp, silver colour shot out from it. It had yellow stripes on a plump black body. A long tongue shot out of his mouth and probed into the opening of the flower. I understood it was collecting something. Golden powder was over his neck and legs. I wondered how he was ever going to clean all of it off. He then flew to the next flower and continued. Then another, identical creature landed near him.

As I looked, more and more of them were moving from one flower to the next. Then I saw something out of the corner of my eye. Shapes with wings larger than those I had just observed, but with feathers that were reminiscent of the eagles. The flying creature I focused on had a bright purple chest and yellow on his wings and a large, long, thin beak, not strong and broad like the eagles.

It darted from side to side, moving swiftly, then hovering. It flapped its wings so fast, they were a blur! Its beak slipped into a large, cup-shaped orange flower, and it drank I watched as its tongue darted in and out as the sticky syrup was taken up.

Wherever I looked, a new and fascinating creature emerged. Wow! Their numbers were endless!

" Yes, Shiloh, there are many creatures and animals in this place, they are all in harmony and exist for the Father's pleasure."

"Where did they all come from and who made them?" I thought.

The teacher grinned and said, "I think you already know the answer to that, young Shiloh."

Yes, I knew. My Father, who had created me, had also created these. Everything, down to the tiniest, smallest detail. I felt so loved at that moment as I remembered Him holding me in the palm of His hand and whispering into my ear. My destiny and my angelic work had started, and even though I did not know what all it would entail, I knew it would be exciting and give my Dad glory.

There were so many things to learn about! Everywhere I looked there was something new. The grass on the ground is different from the grass at home in heaven, here the grass did not sing so beautifully. In fact, as I looked around, everything is a lesser version of home.

Even the light from the enormous ball in the sky is so simple, all it gave out was light and warmth. Not like the glory flowing from the throne, which is the main Light in heaven.

I felt so loved and important, remembering my Father. A tremendous sense of belonging enveloped me. The teacher explained that the ball of light on earth was the sun, and its rays provided a piece in the giant puzzle of life, its job was to light up the world and warm it.

Next, the teacher discussed the difference between the seasons. "There is a season of dryness called summer. Then rain comes to water the earth. The sun lifts yesterday's moisture and makes those fluffy clouds, then releases the moisture as drops of rain. Earth needs it, the plants and trees and the animals need it to live and survive.

At home in heaven, we have the balance of the Father, and we do not need to eat or drink to be sustained, like humans – whom you have yet to see – or the animals do, but we can eat and drink for pleasure. We have angel food. Without food and drink on earth, creatures die.

Not understanding this, we all looked at him. "What's die?" we asked in unison.

"We all live forever," said Ralph. "We are not bound by a concept of time. We can move forwards and backwards. We can be in many places at once. But on earth there is one governing power, time. The Father said it needs to be here as a measure of life on earth. So to die is when that earthly measure, that is allotted to a living body, ends."

It turned out that today I was getting a lot more than a lesson in eagles.

Chapter 3

Humanity's Fate Revealed

The next day, my eagle, who was named Humba, was accompanied by another called Leerooi. Humba kneeled before me and said, " Shiloh, I don't like to get there last!"

He had glistening white feathers on his head, which were waving up and down. Together with the others, he positioned himself at the edge of the portal wall and we all looked on in awe as their feathers changed colour and the eagles were at once camouflaged, disappearing into their surroundings.

I watched as Seymour leaped over the edge of the portal wall and yelled with joy, "Hey-ho Leerooi, I'm coming down."

Leerooi knew Seymour well and had placed himself ready to load his passenger.

I thought I had better follow, but I jumped onto Humba's back with more caution, dived through the cloud and mist opening up into a new realm, and then we lifted high and circled around and around. Soaring high above the clouds, we saw the mountain's peak, standing proud with jagged rocks and steep sides. As we flew over, I saw the Great Hall. Humba saw it too and down we went. Not quite first, but not last either.

The day's lecture began like any other – we students assembled, and I chatted light-heartedly with my classmates. But an air of heightened anticipation charged the pavilion as our esteemed teacher, Ralph, took the stage. After the opening invocation, he scanned us with an intense gaze.

"Students, a new era dawns! The time has come for you to learn of your ultimate purpose here, the reason the Father and all heaven celebrate your creation."

Murmurs rustled through my awed peers at this dramatic opening.

Ralph said, "I know you are burning with questions. You will learn about the Great War, which some of you may have heard about by now. But the most pressing thing right now is to prepare you for your own vital battle ahead!"

My mind raced. Were we destined to be warriors, like Michael's mighty host that dealt Lucifer's rebellion that shattering blow so long ago? I had heard that much, at least. But Ralph then described a mission requiring very different weapons and strategy – guiding a perplexing new creature called mankind back to its Maker and home to the heights of heaven.

I raised my hand, quivering with curiosity.

"Teacher, who is this mankind we must guide? Are they exalted beings that the Father trusts us to escort to him?"

Ralph chuckled at my naïveté.

"Not quite, Shiloh! In fact, compared to beings like ourselves composed of spirit, humanity lives at a diminished capacity – what we'd consider but a shadow existence. Their capacities and perceptions are limited. They dwell on a physical plane, unable to fully perceive spiritual realities."

My classmates and I glanced at each other in puzzled disbelief. Why would the Father extend such effort for these limited creatures' redemption, over other cherished aspects of creation? But before I could frame another question, the air around us began shimmering. A collective gasp escaped our group as the radiant figure of Jesus materialized before us! My heart thrilled at the sudden appearance of heaven's most exalted Prince!

As Jesus smiled warmly upon us, the embroidery of his white tunic flickered like stardust in the ephemeral light.

"Do not underestimate humanity because I chose to envelop myself in mortal flesh to redeem them," he said. "For, mankind plays a pivotal role in the Father's plan for all creation! You see, human souls hold a unique place, created like us in the image of God. Through humanity, the fullest expression of the Father's character and kingdom will be manifested."

Jesus' words revolutionized my perception of mankind's identity. So, their unimposing earthly bodies housed spirits bearing heavenly DNA, as it were! Ralph and the other teachers gazed on as Jesus continued teaching us himself ... how wondrous this was!

"In mankind the Father imparts incredible gifts – creativity, wisdom, mercy, justice, love ... all reflections of Himself looking to flourish further. He yearns for human hearts to embrace goodness and truth, choosing allegiance to Him. For, unlike you angels, born disposed toward obedience, humans must cultivate virtue despite external and internal resistance."

I blinked in dawning understanding of this peculiar contrast – angels obey, but mankind must fight opposition to align their independent wills with the Father's.

Jesus elaborated, "You see, humanity exists in a corrupted state, needing redemption. For, before their first father, Adam, fell to temptation, the rebellious fallen angels infested the earthly plane they were cast into, determined to enslave mankind who was meant to subdue them."

I looked across to Seymour. His eyes were wide, and his ears were stretching towards Jesus as he waited for more.

Jesus continued, "The war resulted from one of the most magnificent angels ever created, thinking he could become greater than the Father. His name was Lucifer. Musical instruments, symbols, pipes and melodies filled Him, and He led the worship in heaven.

When he sang and led the angels in worship before the throne of the Father, all of heaven bowed. They were bowing to the Father and worshipping the Father, but, after some time, Lucifer felt more and more that he could take the Father's place. The Father had given Lucifer a variety of tasks.

He had trained many great angels and felt that he was their idol. This tainted his perception, he felt more important than all the other angels. That is how pride crept into Lucifer's heart and made him feel above the rest: more important, more capable, possessing more authority, more wisdom – in short, better all round.

"Lucifer made a huge mistake. Angels, you have different tasks to do, but you all hold a place before the Father. The great warrior angel, Michael, and his cohorts, they are fierce and mighty, well-seasoned in battle. They cannot swop and do your task, just as you cannot do theirs."

Our class all nodded heads. I felt a great relief, as the thought of fighting was strange to me, and Michael was fierce indeed. I would not like to come up against him!

The entire amphitheater resonated with outraged cries at Lucifer's perverse reversal of roles! Jesus' eyes flashed as he recounted Lucifer and his followers' banishment from heaven after their disastrous failed coup.

"Michael flung them from heaven's heights down to earth's domain, rather than destroy them. Though stripped of access to heavenly glory, these fallen angels retained great power and cunning. When humanity succumbed to sin, it gave the fallen angels license to unleash demonic forces upon Adam and Eve's descendants, who had been created for divine friendship."

I trembled at the thought of this infiltration even of earth by these apostate angels who first abandoned heaven. But Jesus raised a hand to reassure us. "Despite mankind's vulnerability, the Father set in motion their redemption! So, hear and understand your mission: I have overcome the powers of hell on humanity's behalf. But each person must still choose to receive my atoning sacrifice for their rebellion. You guardian angels will guide individuals to salvation through faith, to ultimate union with me."

The realization of serving such pivotal roles in an eternal drama left us awe-struck. We yearned to take up our duties shepherding these human charges away from the demonic underworld's clutches. But Jesus emphasised that we needed Ralph's ongoing leadership, equipping us for the peculiarities of the corporeal dimension we'd be operating in.

"You must learn to operate within its limiting time constraints and perceptions to communicate the spiritual truths, opening their eyes to heaven's reality. There they cannot perceive you, so skill and wisdom are vital in wielding your influence towards redemption.

"So here you are, wondering what it is the Father, and I want you to do. Since the great deception of Lucifer, the Father wants to fill heaven up with true worshippers. But, for truth to prevail, there must be a test. The test is simple and yet hard. It will be possible for each of you to fall into pride – so you must always be on guard and never encourage man to worship you, never lead them to yourselves. Always point them back to Me.

"This creation has many limitations and is bound by many laws and forces that you are above. One of these things is the concept of time. Time is something you have heard about; it is a mechanism that fixes man or animal on a set path.

Three things govern time: the Past, the Present and the Future. These three stages are of the same dimension but cannot exist at the same time. The creatures and plants and even the rocks and water are all affected, and they can only move in one direction, and stay in one time, the present. Present time flows from the past and goes towards the future.

It is important to know that you are not governed by time. You will move from one time to another, past, present, or future, with ease. In fact, you will need to learn the art of using time to help yourselves."

With a blaze of glory, Jesus vanished, leaving us reeling with anticipation of our first descent into earth's unenlightened wilderness, seeking the lost heirs of Eden. Heart pounding, I turned to Ralph as he sought to equip us for an adventure dwarfing our grandest imaginings. Ralph took over from Jesus, saying, "Before you engage earth's darkness, we must cultivate discernment regarding humanity's weaknesses, which provide hell with footholds. The enemy exploits these, to blind people to their feeling of divine belonging. I will educate you about his arsenal of strategies and weapons you must help weak souls resist and escape."

I raised my hand. "Please teacher, expound on the fallen ones' methods. I struggle to grasp their cunning ..."

My classmates murmured agreement at my request.

Sighing, Ralph nodded. "You are right to probe our adversaries' schemes, for these far transcend mere physical violence or coercion. Their cruelty shows itself in mass manipulations of perception, across generations and civilizations!"

We all shuddered at the scope of such social engineering. Ralph described the demons ruthlessly promoting destructive values and customs, contrary to the Father's will.

"In their quest to play god over mankind, they forced mankind to share the earth with them. Nothing delights these fallen angels more than impersonating deities through idol worship."

Seeing our confusion at this concept, Ralph elaborated. "Though deprived of heaven's glories, these demonic spirits retain great power over certain physical forces and abilities, which are beyond ordinary humanity. The people remain oblivious that they are interacting with actual fallen angels masquerading as divine, because of the religious rituals they prescribe."

My righteous indignation stirred at this exploitation of mankind's spiritual longings.

"Why doesn't the Father simply unmake such monsters to keep humanity safe?"

Ralph raised a hand asking for my patience.

"I understand your passion, Shiloh. But only the Most High determines their ultimate fate. For now, these usurpers somehow still cling to existence in their lightless abyss, tirelessly seeking souls to share their exile, by luring them from the truth."

He continued, "So you must see earth swarms with these subverters' demonic progeny from ages past – oppressive ideas, perverted customs, false religions. All of these, blind humanity, who the Father nevertheless determined beforehand would rule this planet. So, through Christ, we must guide them into that spiritual authority and freedom!"

My earlier indignation melted into profound compassion for the deluded victims trapped by the fallen angels.

Ralph roused our courage. "We must honor the Father and King Jesus through the great rescue mission they've granted us a role in! Just as hell targets humanity through matched wits and skill, we must employ studied warfare against its shadow forces. I will train you to operate freely between heaven and earth, to turn souls toward the light!"

We erupted, jumping up with jubilant cheers at Ralph's inspiring exhortation. As I regained my seat, revelations continued dawning in my spirit about the humans we would champion like divine bodyguards. I realized just how deceived these time-bound terrestrial creatures were by the disguises worn by the fallen angels. But we were appointed to be the hosts for heaven-bound spirits, instructed by the Father to guide them through history's darkest storms!

Ralph concluded by unveiling the final crucial truth for grasping our pupils' identity.

"Deep within every man and woman ever conceived beats a spiritual heart, embroidered with eternal glory in the Father's sight. But until they discover its rhythms aligning with heaven's, they will remain lost refugees wandering earth, pursued by sinister ghostly demigods once worshipped by their ancestors. Help them hear redemption's song!"

At last, I grasped why Jesus, and all heaven fortified these outwardly unimpressive beings with mighty guardians – their spirits resonated with the Father's own heartbeat!

Our training ended with Ralph embracing each one of us, weeping with joy. "Go now, dear warrior guides! May your human charges discover within themselves seeds sown from eternity for winning back paradise!"

As the class dispersed, Jesus' last words to me personally resounded within me: "Shiloh, you shall be a prince among these guardian redeemers!" Buoyed with further encouragements, ringing from the cloud of witnesses enveloping heaven's heights, I set my gaze with steely resolution toward the distant, shadowy frontier I would soon pierce to liberate captives. The epic quest awaited!

Chapter 4

Elite Forces Assembled

Ralph stood up and moved in front of other teachers, who were all seated in their console seats. The row of teachers was extensive, as they were preparing many more classes, based on Ralph's teachings. The stage was raised above a huge platform, where thousands of consoles contained line upon line of students holding onto their console controls.

Vibrant colours of information streamed from the screens to the students. We termed this the great download. The lecture we heard that day was important for our understanding of our future charges.

They would need to tap into the instructions of eternity. Our charges were stuck in their bodies and in a three-dimensional understanding of reality. Yes, we understood a lot more, but even our teachers had to keep learning and updating, as our Father continued to create our wonderful Kingdom.

"Class of eighty-four, today we will gain knowledge of how the Father has prepared the power of His word into something that man can use, learn, and understand.

"You may have heard references to the Book, and some of you have seen the effects this Book has on man. The Holy Spirit has endowed man through the ages to write inspired words in manuscripts and scrolls. Various tribes and nations have collected them.

"Certain men, through time, have been able to hear and write the Father's thoughts and words through the inspiration of the Holy Spirit. What they wrote in this book is a collection of all those manuscripts and scrolls. The special messengers of this word were known as prophets, and they had a special and close relationship with the Father."

My curiosity got the better of me, and I asked the console for an example of a prophet. The screen lit up, displaying examples of prophets with their lives in the background. Elijah stood out to me, he was an elderly man with a scraggly beard and greying hair. His skin had wrinkles and blotches and was darker than mine.

Elijah stood before a crowd of 450 angry worshippers of Baal, a god on earth. The god Baal was an entity from the fallen angels. He ruled man with deliberate cruelty and demanded the sacrifice of children and blood. Baal's wife was Asherah, and four hundred of her prophets dined at Queen Jezebel's table. The queen wanted to kill all the prophets of God, and she had succeeded in killing most of them. Only Elijah remained, as he had managed to escape her and her army of prophets.

The scene began with one man, a prophet, who opposed the worship of the Baal god. The jeering grew louder as the worshippers mocked and demanded the prophet's blood.

All of Israel was watching this challenge as it unfolded before them – on one side, a lone prophet representing God the Father, and on the other side, 450 prophets of Baal and 400 Prophets of Asherah. Show-down had begun.

But I heard the conversation between the Father and the prophet.

"Son, you must show my authority. Call them to build an altar to their god and you build an altar to me. And each one of you will call on your God to consume with fire the sacrifice on the altar. I want you to build a moat around the altar and pour water over the slaughtered bulls. Then, I will consume it all with fire to show that I am God and Baal is not."

I saw the prophet challenge the worshippers, and they laughed and danced with joy, in confidence that their god would consume their offerings. They accepted the challenge. The worshippers were agreed and said they would go first and prepare their alter. They were certain that their god would consume their offering with fire.

Two big bulls were brought forward, and Elijah said, "Choose a bull and cut it up into pieces and lay it on a pile of wood. Then call on your god to consume it. I will do the same." Turning to the population of Israel, he said, "Whoever has their god consume their sacrifice, that will be the god you shall follow."

Then I saw Elijah take a huge black bull and slit its throat. It groaned and fell onto its knees and then the big blade swished through the air and struck the neck of the beast, the flesh parted and revealed the blood and muscle, then the blade struck again, and the beast's head was cleaved off the shaking body.

CHAPTER 4

Elijah was veritably washed in the blood of the bull, and as it dried, it formed streaks along his face and body, and his piercing eyes were busy taking in the frustrations of the other prophets, as they danced around, making a grand show of things.

They lifted up their bull's heart and raised it in mock offering to their deity. The drummers were beating the drums feverishly and a group of women dancers came out and writhed around. All seemed to serve the show of things, to keep the huge crowd occupied.

The butchering was long and hard work for Elijah – the prophet cleaved the bull in half and into pieces and laid it on a pile of wood, between twelve large stones that represented the tribes of Israel. Then he laid the meat from the bull on top of the wood and dug a moat around the whole altar.

He then ordered the servants to pour 4 jars of water onto the meat and drench the wood. He told them to repeat the process 3 times. The water ran over the wood and filled the moat.

I heard worshippers chanting and saw them dancing before a giant statue of Baal. They were sacrificing babies to appease its hunger for young blood. This caused the rock to have dark stains, where the blood would run down to be collected by the priests and then consumed in ceremonies to worship Baal.

The priests were getting desperate now as they twirled around in a frantic dance. Still nothing. I could see that six hours had passed, and the sun was now passing the midday mark in the sky. They were now cutting themselves with blades and calling out to their god to come down and consume the sacrifice, but nothing happened.

"Maybe your god is having a sleep," said Elijah.

They stopped and looked back at the grinning prophet and then continued with more zeal than before. I chuckled and looked up from my console to see Seymour grinning back at me.

I became aware that Ralph had continued lecturing, as my attention was drawn back into the console. But again, I was distracted by the scenes still playing out on my screen.

The prophets of Baal were in despair. Evening had come and still nothing had happened. Then Elijah stood up, raised his arms, and asked God to consume the sacrifice.

The fire of the Lord came down and consumed the offering, the wood and dust and even licked up all the water in the trench.

Then Elijah commanded all the 450 prophets to be taken to the brook at Kishon and be executed there.

I was still holding the joystick of the console. I had been riveted by the scene, I could still smell the burnt meat and hear the cries from the desperate prophets as they were executed.

Now my attention reverted back to our teacher Ralph, who was waving his arms around and being his usual expressive self. Hoping, I thought, to keep everyone's attention, well, not everyone's. Feeling a little guilty, I quickly tuned back into Ralphs lecture.

"The enemy has tried to pollute and destroy these words. He uses many ways of doing this, but one of his most effective ways is to use man's wish to be self-sufficient and independent from the Father. When man leaves the Father's protection and authority of his own free will, he opens himself to the enemy. The enemy will use individuals or groups of people to destroy others.

"But, when a man takes heed of the words in this Book, he will be under the Father's protection. You, as guardians, will help man get home much more easily if he is familiar with the Word of God. If man turns his back on the Father, then he is also turning his back on any help from the power in the Book."

Ralph lifted the book high above his head, it had a leather cover, but being alive, the colours danced and changed, and words flew out and swirled. Sometimes they would hover in front of a student, then shoot back into the book.

"The Kingdom has certain keys that are available to man to use and unlock that power. The knowledge and understanding of the Book is one of those keys. That is why the enemy attacks the use of the Book. He will make it sound old, outdated information and man will find it a battle to read.

"There is a network of angels to aid man. Man can find explanations for everything he is exposed to in his daily life in this Book of empowering knowledge. If man can master the power in the Book, he will have the advantage of overcoming the traps and ploys of the enemy. Physical and emotional forces rule his realm, but man can be immersed into his environment to enjoy the creation the Father has provided for him to enjoy and thrive in.

"The enemy planted negative emotions to break man, not to benefit man," he added.

Without warning, the book cracked with a loud rumbling sound, a voice roared and said "Son, make me an altar and sacrifice a bull on it ... "

I felt a strange warmth and glow on my cheeks as the Father's voice repeated what I had already heard. Ralph looked over at me with a grin and said, "I wonder who knows this story."

CHAPTER 4

I assumed that I was being asked to relate it and was about to tell the hundreds of startled students, but as I began raising my hand, with some caution, a gruff and familiar voice interjected, from the side of me.

"Well, I can say," said Seymour, "that was when prophet Elijah had a challenging day." He cleared his throat and chuckled, "You do remember, don't you, Ralph, that we were on an assignment there and had the adventure of our lives." He started to elaborate, as the whole school leaned in to hear all the details.

But Ralph cleared his throat and said, "We don't need to elaborate now, Seymour, these young uns just need to know that one day they, too, will have a great adventure.

"Sin," he continued, "which is an act that opposes the Father's Kingdom, has intertwined itself with every facet of man's life. He faces temptations every day, and when he allows the temptation to win and to ensnare him, he has committed sin. Jesus came to man's realm. He lived the life of man but never fell to the temptation of sin. He accepted all of man's sin and enabled man to be pardoned by His death on the cross.

"I will teach you more about how to help your charge to find and use the Book to get him home. But that is for another lesson," said Ralph.

"I would like to find that book," I thought, but my thought was interrupted once again by the familiar voice of his friend Seymour.

"You have the book in your memory, Shiloh, and you have the deep understanding of it that man must seek throughout his whole life. You will never forget the truth and will always know what to say or do to help your charge. The difficulty lies with the charge, who has free will. He needs to make every decision on his own and will reap the rewards, or the destructive consequences of the choices he makes. We can only guide him."

Ralph paced before us, his brow furrowed in concern.

"My students, you must understand – sin has infected every part of the mortal realm. It lurks around every corner, waiting to tempt and ensnare humanity."

He paused, meeting each of our gazes.

"Imagine your charge, let's call her Ava. She wakes, eager to start her day. After morning prayers, she makes breakfast for her family. But the savoury bacon triggers a craving – she takes more than her share, ignoring the needs of her siblings."

Ralph shook his head. "It's a small act of selfishness, but it's sin, nonetheless. It creeps in wherever it can. Later, say, on her walk to school, Bobby, a fellow student, rushes by and knocks Ava's books out of her hands. Hot anger flares up inside her, and she screams insults after him."

I nodded, beginning to understand how these 'sins' could entrap someone.

"At lunch, jealousy pricks when Ava's friend receives a gift from her boyfriend. Then comes dishonesty, when Ava peeks at another's test ..."

Ralph raised his hands. "Her soul is beset on all sides. Our Jesus lived a sinless life among such temptations, then sacrificed himself to save humanity from them. This gift has been recounted over and again.

"The enemy uses every trick – greed, pride, lust – to mislead our charges, as he has corrupted the mortal realm in his image."

I saw many nods of agreement. Many of the angels had witnessed such deception firsthand.

"He twists relationships, making comrades into rivals. He provokes hostilities between families, races, nations. All to sow hatred and chaos."

Murmurs rose as my fellow guardians recalled specific instances of the enemy's schemes.

Ralph went on, "He infests institutions and public places – schools, governments, marketplaces – to spread injustice."

Seymour added, "I have seen him poison minds at all levels of society. No one is immune to his influence."

Ralph nodded. "Even the innocent is vulnerable," he said. "He lures away children with false promises. He incites youth to abandon faith and family."

"I've watched him trap many in addictions that destroy lives," one young angel growled, fists clenched.

Listening in on the edges of the pavilion, Humba flapped his wings in agitation. "He imprisons so many in cycles of violence and retribution," he cried.

The anger in the circle was palpable. But Ralph raised his hands in a calming gesture. "As long as we stand together, he cannot win! Our charges find strength in us and the light we carry from here."

My fellow guardians rose, recognizing the truth of his words. Ralph raised his hands for silence and continued.

"Yes, we must guide humanity through darkness. But we do not walk alone – the Father arms us with courage and wisdom."

I nodded to both my mentors, Ralph and Seymour. They smiled kindly in return.

"And when our charges complete their journeys," Ralph concluded, "we rejoice together in triumph. Their resilient spirits are a testament to the Father's love."

I gazed around at my comrades, my heart swelling with hope.

"So let us rally together," I spoke aloud, "united by devotion. We are the Father's instruments, ushering His children home."

Thunderous applause erupted. My mentors applauded. Humba whooped and took flight in a celebratory loop.

For, we were indeed guardians united by love – guiding humanity through darkness into the Father's eternal light. Our mission was clear, and with it came immeasurable joy.

We left the lecture hall, uplifted by a greater understanding of our role. And also, a sense of adventure awaited.

Chapter 5

A Perfect Paradise Lost

Here we were, all together, with a great feeling of anticipation. I had been told by Seymour that this was going to be the most exciting lesson we had had so far. I wondered about this, as he wore a funny grin and winked at me.

Sometimes I wondered if I understood him, but, looking around me at the other guardians, I soon realised that all their mentors had hinted that what we about to experience was a highly rated exhibition.

The entire class was eager to learn and lined up.

"We are going on your first observation tour," said Ralph.

"This is a special and important excursion. I want you to be extra observant. We will witness the beginning of man. The Father will, further, allow you to see the fall of man. This is pivotal to your understanding of how the world has fallen so low.

"When we enter upon the realm of man, understand that most cannot see you. Sometimes the Father will grant to you an understanding of what man is thinking. In the heavenly realm, we can often communicate by thoughts, but this is not so on earth. Man has lost this skill.

"Class, the Father made the earthly realm for the benefit of man. He wanted somewhere for man to walk alongside Him. The Father wanted man to be His companion and friend. Some of you are wondering why the Father would even need or want another to be His friend. Well, He is a good Father and made man in His image. He wanted relationship and fellowship with humanity, because He loved that which He had created.

"Man was given a pristine environment, to rule over everything that the Father had created. But the fallen army of Lucifer also existed in this realm and the second heaven. The Father and all the angels and creatures of heaven had their abode in the third heaven. But the fallen angels hated God and his whole creation and reasoned amongst themselves that they would hurt the Father through His creation of man.

"However, the Father knew what was coming and had prepared a great army. Man's enemy was thrown out of the third heaven to earth, the first heaven, where he still wages war on humanity, wishing to destroy him by encouraging him to rob life, kill, steal and in general destroy the blessings that the Father had planned for His creation. Lucifer tries to turn man against God.

"We are part of heaven's army and there are over three times the number of good angels, compared with the ones that were thrown out. The evil angels who lost are now called fallen angels. Neither they nor Lucifer will ever be allowed to return to the third heavenly realm, and this makes Lucifer mad!

"At times, we are commanded by the archangel Michael, who you spoke to, Shiloh, on that first day. Michael is a mighty warring angel, but even he must submit to the authority and command of the Father. The son of the Father is an important member of the three-part Godhead. He is the top commander. He is called the 'LORD of hosts'."

Seymour grinned at me and said, "You still have not told us what Michael said to you. I bet it was encouraging and exciting."

Seymour's grin could not be contained. He already knew what the Archangel Michael had said, but he just 'liked to have sport,' as he put it.

Ralph interrupted our banter.

"OK, settle down, you two, you will have plenty of time to chat later. Right now, concentrate on everything you see and hear and smell. I want you to start using your senses much more. You will need to be on guard, as the enemy will know we are watching. He won't be able to harm you, but today you will see him for the first time."

A strange feeling rose in me. The feeling had so much energy and made the colours swirl. The feeling, as I soon came to know, was excitement. Whenever this arose in me, it was an indicator of stimulating things to come. It heightens all my senses, which became attuned in anticipation, and then I knew I was in alert mode. I glanced at Seymour, who was grinning again.

"You feel it, hey! It is the greatest. We are going to see something new and exhilarating."

Ralph continued, "We are going to go there to witness the great fall of man. You cannot interfere, you will only be able to observe. Class, this is the turning point of your existence, today you will have your heart and minds opened to the truth. It will shake you, but also give you the understanding you will need to accomplish your task for the Father. He wants you to be the best, and my job is to show you everything I can to help you. I feel you are now ready to see the first encounter.

"Now, I want you to pair up with someone and then line up at portal No.1."

Seymour came over to me with a big smile.

"I don't think you want to be down there all alone. Shiloh, you and I will work together. If you will have me?" he said, bowing down before me and holding his open hand across his broad chest. The white robe glistened, and I glimpsed a silver mantle under the robe. The weave in the mantle danced. As I watched, the mantle disappeared back into Seymour's white skin. Seymour was beaming, with that unmistakable twinkle in his eye. He leaned forward and said,

"I will help to get you one, your own mantle. These are not just for anyone. They are seriously cool."

Something seemed to jump inside me as Seymour put his powerful arm around me and guided me towards the edge of the portal. He was a good twelve inches taller than me and a lot broader. He had well-defined muscles and brawny hands. My shape was slender and my hands graceful, my fingers were long compared to his chunky fingers, which looked like they could grab hold of anything and never let go.

He read my thoughts and said, "Well, young un, they are for gripping, not much will get away from these." He lifted his hands up and waved them around like they were paddles.

We moved towards portal number one. An edge rose out of the ground and formed a barrier both physical and surreal, forming a wall which was up to my belly and stretching in a circle about a mile wide.

As I watched, the inside of the walled circle closed in and then opened again. It seemed to breathe. Angels of all types were diving over the edge. Some had armour on, while others were dressed more like the teacher.

They had groups of young ones with them. So, there are other classes, I thought.

"Of course, there are," said Seymour. "We are just one class among many. We are not the largest group of angels, either. There are multitudes of us. Angels have different roles, such as carrying provisions, building, and causing breakthrough and deliverance. Today, we are here to observe not only man, but also how the realms interact. There are many types of angels, but one universal reason why we have been created is that, beyond worshipping the Father, we are to help man. Understand this: we obey the Father on the throne. Our assignments are from Him, but He has made us all ministering spirits to give aid to man on the earth – because Lucifer tries to keep man separated from the Father. Our task is to work together to help bring man's soul back to the Father. We respond to the prayers of man. We can be triggered, because of his words that he declares upon the earth. You shall learn that some have had their spiritual senses exercised to such a degree that they can interact with us – that is most enjoyable! It will also be much needed in the days to come."

Humba and Leerooi appeared, and Seymour and I had the same idea again. We jumped over the wall and landed on our rides, Humba and Leerooi. We still had to wait for the rest of the class to mount up. Ralph looked at us and grinned.

When he lifted his arm and brought it down again, we all, in perfect formation, banked left, then right, then straight down. The sky appeared to be full of brown darts, heading in the same direction. Humba was communicating with his companions. He glanced back at me and said,

"Just hold on, we are going to pass through."

Pass through what? I thought. This was going to be different from my first visit to earth.

Suddenly, we were in a mist that grew thicker, until it was obscuring our vision. Strange smells wafted past as we held on tight. I realised the smells revealed we were approaching the earthly realm I'd already been introduced to, filled with amazing creatures and plants. The closer we came, the stronger the aromas were. Humba was a great flight master, and he could pinpoint a spot in the dark and fly straight to it. He also could feel that I was tense. He spoke to my mind and said, "Young un, you enjoyed the journey down last time, didn't you? It always means adventure. This place of man is a shadow of our home, it has its challenges, but it is always exciting."

The mist thinned, and we popped out the other end — into a different realm from the one I'd been exposed to the previous time.

Ralph had adjusted our interaction sensors.

We angels have acute senses, and a great range in our sensory perception. But Ralph wanted us to experience an equivalent experience to man's.

So now we could smell in a similar way as man smells and, also, our hearing was tweaked. It could be returned to our own settings by ourselves and I remember jumping from one setting to the next and discovering that man has a rather small capacity – even less than the animals that he is supposed to have authority over. Some of the odours seemed to sit in the back of my throat and I could taste the aroma.

This was a bit unusual, compared to what I was used to. Other smells were not nice at all, but this was man's world, and I was on an adventure of discovery.

The sun was warm, and the sounds of birds were almost deafening. Animals roamed everywhere. I now know that blue sky and unfamiliar smells, smells I now know are of earthy nature, the trees and vegetation, gave off different fragrances. Some were sweet, and others were heavy and strong. Besides, of course, all the animals I observed gave off their own aromas, which seemed to flow over me. Wow, it was beautiful, and huge. As far as the eye could see, there were rolling hills, mountains, trees, and green grass.

Ralph said that this was comparable to our realm.

He was standing next to his eagle. He always seemed to get to his destination before anyone else. Seymour swooped in next, then landed beside me. Ralph was still speaking as I glanced at Humba, who grinned and shrugged "Well, this is not the first flying job for me."

Ralph interjected in a rather authoritative tone,

"Now pay attention, all of you," he said. "We are here as observers, so we cannot interact or interfere with what we shall see. We are going to see the fall of man. Jesus Himself has already told you about it, now you will witness it first-hand. The enemy you have heard so much about will be here, and he will cause the fall through trickery. This is his favourite ploy. He is proud and arrogant, he pretends to be God here, and he wants to hurt the Father and the Father's creation. All he can do is destroy and corrupt. He can never create.

"The enemy will see you today and try to intimidate you. Do not react to or show any aggression or react to them. Remember, we are only here on the observation platform. This actual event took place 6000 years ago in earth time. We, as you now know, are not bound by time as the world is, but we can traverse in any direction and observe unique events, which will help you understand why man thinks and behaves the way he does," Ralph said.

Then – there they were, the first two humans, a woman and a man! Walking in a beautiful garden, tall trees reached up to the sky and made a canopy, like a ceiling. Filtered light came down to the ground. In some patches it was bright, others dim, making moving patterns that seemed to sway back and forth.

We heard them speaking and laughing together. A large lion walked beside them, and the man's hand was resting on his head and seemed to stroke him.

The lion was enjoying it. The woman pointed up to the tree, where a blue and gold bird was singing to his less eye-catching mate. He danced along the branch and twirled and jumped up and down. All the while, he was singing a beautiful song.

This was all for the benefit of his bride, who was loving the attention, but was pretending to be a little put out by it all. This only made the male bird more determined to capture her notice. He rose higher in the air and turned and landed and rose again. We, the angels, all watched along with Adam and Eve. Eve was Adam's companion. While she reflected a unique part of creation, together they merged into one.

Ralph told us how the Father had created Eve out of Adam's rib and breathed His life into her. She was to be Adam's helper and companion, and together they were to take dominion of the earth, cause it to be fruitful and rule over it. God gave them this ability when He created them in His image, His likeness.

Adam and Eve stood awhile, looking at the bird's efforts, then Adam said to the female bird,

"If you don't encourage him a bit, he will lose interest and fly off to find another mate."

The female bird looked at Adam and said,

"Oh, he is so magnificent. I don't want him to stop dancing just yet."

The angels all laughed, and Adam and Eve continued to walk, so caught up with each other that they were oblivious to the large company of angels watching.

"Now, class, Adam can communicate with all the animals and birds," said Ralph. "He has a deep understanding about their behaviour, and the Father even asked him to name every single one."

"So, they can't see us right now?" asked another guardian angel who was standing nearby. His name was Cosmos. Cosmos looked more like Seymour than me. He was strong and had braided hair that glistened in the sunlight. It was a white shade of grey and he had threaded gold through the braids to keep them in place. His robes were more detailed than mine, as he was from another class and had graduated from the first stage. This particular excursion was so popular, however, so many classes attended, including graduates.

Ralph smiled, glad that some of his older students were still inquisitive and said,

"That's right, Cosmos. They are oblivious to us right now. The lion can see us, so can the birds. In fact, all the animals can sense us and sometimes see us. But man cannot. Well, only when The Father permits it, then they will see. Listen! The Father is coming now."

We heard Him walking in the garden. He appeared by the tall yellowwood tree. The tree was tall and it towered above the canopy. The Father's Presence appeared next to the tree, which seemed to diminish in its posture of greatness, next to my wonderful Father. His Presence filled the air and rays of bright Light streamed forth in every direction. The leaves in the surrounding woodland trembled with awe and the birds all rose and spun around, dancing. Unspeakable joy filled every part of the Father's creation.

"Hello Adam, Hello Eve," He said, in a loving voice. They embraced one another and He shared their joy in the bird's grand display. They wandered down the path together, their laughter filling the air, and a beautiful fragrance lingered.

Ralph explained, "The Father comes down to speak with Adam, and they discuss many things. The Father takes great delight in hearing how Adam sees things and how he would do things. Adam has a special place in the Father's heart. The Father could have named all the animals and creatures, but He has given Adam dominion over the world. This is Adam's world.

"There is absolute freedom for Adam here, and he can do whatever he wants to. Adam has the luxury of walking around the garden and dictating how things should grow. He is highly creative, actually. Adam had instructed the giant climbing rose to cover the grand arch you see here. The rose emits a wonderful fragrance that fills the air, while he and Eve sit and watch the animals come down to drink," continued Ralph.

"Here, along the river, are rows of trees, each producing fresh fruit. Some fruits are small and brightly coloured. Some are round, others are more like drops of water. There are many forms of fruit that are edible, and by eating the fruit, Adam and Eve grow strong, and they relish the experience of eating, just as the animals and birds do.

"Some of the fruit has stone-like pips, which are the seeds that find their way into the ground, and grow into a tree just like the one they fell from – for they create after their own kind. Some seeds are small, and the birds and other animals actually do a great job of planting them.

"You see, class, the animals and birds and even the stars in the sky at night, are all here, making for the richness of this creation, for Adam and Eve to enjoy. Everything works together for the good of man.

"The Father has planned everything down to the most minute detail. Animals multiply and know how to raise their offspring, how to feed and look after each other. The birds lay eggs that contain a replica of the parent birds. There are many types of each animal and many species. There are also creatures who live in the rivers and seas, but that will be explained in our third tour.

"Right now, I want you to observe the wonderful relationship that man has with the place he calls home, and his relationship with the Father.

"Here they are, walking together and talking. The Father asks Adam to tell Him everything, and they discuss many future projects. The Father comes down every day, and laughter fills their home. You will come to know that a particularly wonderful feeling comes with this fruit of laughter. In fact, we angels, and other creatures from our home, grow excited when the Father calls on Adam. It seems all creation reacts to the union and fellowship of the Father and man," said Ralph.

"The colours around Adam and the Father dance and shoot out and cover other parts of the garden. A fragrance, deliciously sweet and tangible, accompanies the colours and mingles into everything. The animals especially like it. They jump and shake their heads about and dance and show off to each other how high they can twirl.

"Unlike in our home,' he continued, there is a force here called gravity. It holds everything in its place, and that place is the ground. If some fruit is let go by the tree, it will fall to the ground and bounce and roll until the fruit comes to a resting spot. The beings here can push against this, but it takes what we know as energy to push back. That is why the animals jump, as if to beat the force of gravity," said the teacher.

"Man, and all the life forms in this realm need to eat to sustain themselves. They eat fruit, for example, and that is converted into energy in the body and the body grows. They then have the energy to walk and run and jump. We do not have to eat, as we have the Father's energy. In our realm, we do not need food.

"In man's kingdom, as you know, they have a concept called time, and the Father links time to the ageing process. Man does not live here forever. He has a determined amount of time in this realm to complete the works that the Father has prepared for him to do. When he has completed this work, he moves out of his physical body and is in the spirit again – just as he was with the Father before he was born and came down to this realm. Man grows from an infant or baby to a child and then into an adult. After some time, he ends his days here as an old and, hopefully, wise man.

"You are angels and don't age or have the troubles of a temporary body. And you, of course, will never die because your bodies are pure Spirit. Right now, as you watch the Father and Adam and Eve, they are in perfect harmony. They share their thoughts, and Adam is incredibly wise and asks the Father many intricate questions. The Father always answers him, and they discuss many varied subjects. It is perfect watching the flow of the words. You will notice, class, as the Father speaks, the words create, and if Adam wants something, the Father will weigh up the consequences and, if it is good, he will create it.

"Adam once asked the Father, could the Father change a flat lake into something more thrilling? Shiloh, you are looking at the result –This is known as a waterfall. It's magnificent, isn't it? There are more of these, and they all have a special place in Adam's dance for Eve. Yes, like the male bird, he likes to show off to Eve. His favourite thing is to climb to the top of a waterfall and call to Eve, then he will launch himself like an eagle and dive from the falls into the blue lake beneath. Eve giggles and gets all excited and dives into the lake and swims out on a porpoise to meet him. The porpoise is a water creature, which they ride. Adam has even been seen to stand up on the back of the porpoise and command it to leap out of the water, sometimes they even do somersaults together," said Ralph, smiling, as even the memory of this playful interaction between Adam and Eve and the creation invariably brought joy to all.

I saw the Father turning to Adam, embracing him and saying, "You carry on, son, you are doing a wonderful thing here."

Smiling tenderly at Eve, he said, "Eve, you are a complement to Adam, you make him whole, and that pleases Me so much."

We watched as waves of love vibrated between them all.

They said their farewells, and the Father walked towards the large yellowwood tree. The sky shimmered and reflected the intense Light of the Father until we could no longer see, so bright was that Light. When our vision returned, we no longer saw His Presence.

Our attention moved to a magnificent willow tree, whose branches fell towards the water's edge like a curtain of green. There it parted, and the enemy appeared. He looked menacing and powerful, his eyes dark and deep. He was followed by numerous angels like himself, the fallen ones. These angels had once been formidable and strong. Now they walked in a sly, stooped fashion. Everything about them looked menacing and slippery, they even bickered amongst each other, shuffling for position to be near their master.

CHAPTER 5

Seymour grabbed my arm and whispered, "That is him, the one they call Lucifer. He used to be magnificent and had all the created ones in heaven following his music. When he played, everything stopped to listen. Look at him move with cunning and purpose."

The joyful and peaceful atmosphere had vanished, and had been replaced by an edgy darkness. No longer was the light ablaze. Even the colours on the water had changed to a duller, grey tone. The air seemed cooler, ominously chill.

We, the class on this trip, became the silent onlookers of the excursion, listening as Lucifer spoke to the Father's beloved ones.

"Hello Adam, hello Eve, is this not a wonderful day? All of creation seems to bow before you. Why, even the Father thinks you are great and mighty. Eve, the Father, seems to be especially pleased with how you make Adam so complete. Look at all this: you have been busy. That falling water was not here the last time I was here. Did you create it?" he asked.

As I observed this tense interaction, my attention was riveted to every movement this intruder made, and I could see Adam felt the same. He shifted from side to side. Clearly, he did not like Lucifer and his wayward band of angels. Apparently they were not always around, but appeared from time to time. This unsettled Adam somewhere deep down. He did not feel joy around these angels.

Without waiting for a reply, Lucifer continued, "So, what has the Father been discussing with you today? I have heard Him laugh and smelled that smell. Yes, Adam, I know what it is like to be in the presence of the Father. So, come now, what were you talking about? Hmmm, let us see. I saw him talking about that great enormous tree over there."

Lucifer pointed out a great apple tree. As the class looked on, we sensed something was not quite right, but did not understand what was unfolding before us.

"It is a special tree, is it not, Eve? Why, Adam, you are the co-creator with the Father here in the garden, you can do whatever you like," said Lucifer. "Eve, surely the Father has said you can eat of the fruit of every tree in the garden?"

We heard Eve reply, "Yes, we may eat the fruit of the trees in the garden but of that one tree in the midst – we must not eat its fruit, nor even touch it, or we will die!"

Lucifer continued, "Surely not! You know, don't you, that if you eat that fruit, you will be just as wise and knowledgeable as the Father? Just think of it, no more questions, because you will know everything. Surely the Father will be pleased with this, and you both can just create new things and not waste your time on all those queries and discussions."

We watched as the deceiver planted the lie into the minds of Adam and Eve. We saw how the words pierced and twisted into them, as sharp as arrows spiralling deep down into their hearts. And new thoughts spread through them and, as Eve was filled, she saw the fruit of that tree would be good to eat.

"He is right, you know, Adam, we need to know everything." With that, she picked the fruit.

Lucifer leaned forward and smiled at Eve and said, "I believe it to taste like satisfaction itself. Yes, you will be truly complete."

She bit off a chunk and chewed. The juice dribbled down the side of her mouth, and Adam looked on longingly, wondering how it could be wrong, if Eve enjoyed it so much?

I watched Adam lean towards Eve as he tried to smell the aroma of the fruit. He knew every fruit had its own smell. Some were sweet, and others were pungent, and some even smelled horrible. This fruit's fragrance caused his nostrils to flare with anticipation. Intense, perfumed spices filled the air and I could see the swirling of all the colours as the smell penetrated his inner being.

His thoughts were enticing him, I knew that the perfume and the promises attached to the fruit were too much for Adam, and when Eve gave him the fruit, he put it to his lips without thinking, and the succulent aroma overcame him.

As Adam bit down into the fruit, I felt like leaping through the gap and grab the fruit from his hands. I experienced a mixture of betrayal, rebellion, jealousy, and pride – similar to what Adam and Eve felt. Adam chewed, all the while looking at Eve, hoping he was not too late. In his eyes, Eve must not be wiser than he. Then it happened.

The ground shook, and the trees fell silent. All the birds looked at each other differently. The lion suddenly had the desire to eat meat, not just the fruit, but to eat live deer. Beasts turned on each other.

Death had entered, and the chase began. They all ran from or after each other. Confusion abounded. Suddenly, the pure light of day was dimmed. A fierce wind woke up and howled and blew so hard that the branches of the large yellowwood tree rocked violently, and the whole tree crashed to the ground.

The loudest sound, however, was cackling laughter from Lucifer and the fallen ones.

They were shouting, "It has begun! We are kings here and will rule and reign on earth. It is ours. It has been given to us by man and we will take it all! The beginning has started."

With that, they departed through a swaying, weeping willow tree. The branches seemed to lash out at the water as if to rid it of its place at the foot of the mighty tree. Adam looked around, and Eve shrank into his chest. They now tasted fear for the first time, and it gripped them. Everything had changed, they had changed and, what was worse, they now understood too much and knew they had done something wrong.

I have learned about deception and the thirst for power at all costs, I thought. How this would run havoc through Adam's life and his descendants was something we would never forget. Ralph's observation settings allowed me to feel Adam's emotions and the pain of deception.

Adam and Eve had disobeyed the Father and His command and thus they had broken their world and their promise to the Father never to eat of that particular tree.

Adam knew he could not undo it. He had lost all his rights in the garden, and nothing would obey him anymore. The lion would not listen when he told him to stop chasing the gazelle, and the wind did not quieten down at his command, but seemed to bellow back, mocking him.

Many other thoughts were now being sent like arrows by the fallen ones into Adam and Eve. A riot of confusion and fear assaulted them, but, worst of all, Adam now realised that he had lost his special place with the Father.

We watched as Adam collapsed to the ground, holding his head in agony with both hands, as a new emotion, called grief, enveloped him and he sobbed, his big wet tears falling into the earth that had once helped form him. Now there was no such communion with life, as of the breath of the Father, which had breathed into him. We saw the earth reject his tears and cry out with great groanings, for now it was condemned also, as all creation, to the creeping shadow of death, which emerged to rule.

All harmony had fled. Death reigned through Adam. Even though we angels were of another creation, we felt for the first time a deep, dark feeling of despair.

"Now, class," we heard Ralph's voice summon our attention, "the feeling you are having is just a taste of what Adam and Eve are feeling. You have been permitted to feel what they felt, so that you can have some sort of gauge of what is really happening. You cannot always tell what is going on from outside appearances. Man has many levels. He is now feeling these thoughts for the first time. He knows for sure is that he has disobeyed the Father. He comprehends that it is not pleasant for him to have this knowledge of good and evil, that it changes everything henceforth. Even the display of the animals has changed – as you see, they do not obey him anymore. The whole balance of the Creation has shifted."

As Ralph explained the situation, my stomach was churning, and my mind raced, as all these ideas flashed in front of my thought screen. These excuses, the thought came, and next, blame. Yes, blame Lucifer, I thought. It was, after all, his idea.

"Yes, man will now feel those thoughts, Shiloh," said Ralph, reminding me that these thoughts were a part of my education.

We all watched as Adam and Eve slunk away to an overhanging rock, as the wind howled and branches smashed to the ground. We watched as Adam tried one last time to gain back some of the authority he had once had.

Raising his voice as loudly as he could, he screamed, "Lie down and be still!" But the wind, no longer under his influence, cracked a large branch and flung it vengefully back at Adam. Adam leapt out of the way and retreated into the cave. A few minutes before, Adam had not hesitated to order the wind to abate, but now he felt useless and powerless. He knew he had lost everything.

The garden grew darker and everywhere the bushes and trees rustled, and the animals and birds called out in desperation as night drew in. Adam grew cold and held the shivering Eve to his chest. He reached over and grabbed a large banana leaf and covered both as they lay down to try to sleep. They did not sleep or even dare discuss what had taken place. They both dreaded meeting the Father the next day. Inwardly, they both also doubted one another, as thoughts and feelings of distrust took advantage and crept in.

"Class, we may find the concept of disobedience and betrayal strange, but it is not unknown in our creation," Ralph's voice interjected. "Remember that Lucifer did just that to the Father? He betrayed the Father's trust in him, and he paid a permanent price. Lucifer was removed from the throne room and cast down to this realm. He is no longer granted entrance to the highest heavenly realm, the Heaven of heavens.

"This is not only about Adam's sin in disobeying the Father. It is about the consequences of action. The Father had grand plans for a wonderful life for Adam. Now that has changed, as sin and death are passed on from generation to generation."

We remained in the earthly realm until morning broke through with a loud rumble, and the ground shook. This time, the Father was striding with purpose and determination. The animals moved away, and the wind stood still. Nothing moved, all was silent.

"Adam, where are you? Adam!" the Father spoke with a stern, knowing voice.

Adam took away the large leaf covering his own and Eve's body and reached over to a branch above him, from which he and Eve plucked several leaves, putting them together to cover themselves.

CHAPTER 5

Adam grabbed Eve's hand and they walked out to meet the Father, who was standing in a great clearing, waiting. They were both timid and shaking, experiencing terrible feelings of emptiness and despair. Even so, the sun was shining and order had returned to the garden. Even the lion was calm, though the gazelle kept a watchful eye.

The Father said, "Adam, what have you done? Do you understand now what I tried to tell you? Now you see it, don't you? Why did you do it?"

Adam blurted out, "But – Eve!"

Father then gave Eve a chance to explain herself also, "Woman, what have you done?"

She said, "The serpent, Lucifer, deceived me!"

With that, the Father sadly shook his head. He knew Adam had changed and that now he needed to be banished from the garden. As we listened and watched, we knew the Father felt the pain of the separation. He made Adam and Eve garments from animal skin to clothe them and protect them from the heat of the sun and the cool of the night.

Then, on command of the Father, two Cherubim angels flew in and drew fiery swords and walked towards Adam and Eve, who backed up towards the garden's gateway. Huge stone walls rose to the tops of the trees, and a large, barred gate swung open.

Beyond the gate, where Adam had never been, things looked harsh and uninviting. The two fugitives looked back at the Father, who looked past them and said,

"You will toil out there, Adam, for now the ground is cursed and you will not have dominion as before. Now you will work upon the earth. But my love for man is so strong that my plan still stands. I will have a people who choose to love Me, and I will make a way for them to search for Me with all their hearts, and when they do, they shall surely find Me."

These words followed Adam and Eve out into the wilderness. The Father watched as his special companion walked, broken and shamed, into the distance.

A stillness hung in the air as creation waited, then the Father slowly turned and moved towards the portal and said out loud, so all in the garden could hear,

"Close the Gates! Do not let them back in! This garden is now sectioned off until such a time as I ordain."

With that, all the animals and birds also left the garden and wandered or flew out into the wilderness. The Gates swung shut with a deafening clang and large angels stood guard. The animals, too, became cautious and afraid of the new land, which brought all kinds of new challenges. Every animal knew why the change had happened.

They seemed to know by instinct that their existence was now going to depend on their wits, and they, too, were going to have to fight for every bit of life or die.

Desperation, fear, anxiety, shame, hurt, and more dark feelings multiplied and swarmed over the land, as if dancing in weird delight they had won and had been given authority to torment mankind in this new world, which they now had rule over.

In the many ranks of watchers, we stood in silence. We all expected the situation would change back to the original, but the heaviness stayed.

Ralph said, "Now, you have witnessed the fall of man. This is, as Lucifer said, the start of the new age, but it is also one of the reasons why we are here. Our job is to help bring man back to the Father and regain what Adam and Eve lost. You have witnessed how easily Adam and Eve were robbed of their birthright. We have a vast job now to do, as we must bring man back to the Father one by one."

"So, we end this excursion. We will have many more encounters with man's past to help you understand his position in the realms. Mount up and head back to the portal."

Chapter 6

Dark Powers Arising

The next day was to be the most important but also the most eye-opening lesson we had ever had.

It was a normal day at school, and we all assembled in the great hall. The tall pillars were full of moving scenes, flashing in a myriad of vibrant colours, colours swirling out of one pillar, to be sucked into another.

The colour waves carried words that intertwined and impregnated a screen on another pillar. It became a game for the students to guess what the lecture would be whenever the screens erupted. We knew in part, as we managed a few glimpses of the moving scenes. But today was too much – there were too many bolts of light, too many voices, too much for even our advanced inner selves to be able to determine a subject.

Ralph was up in front with several other teachers. As we assembled to be assigned our lessons for the day, we intuited that it was going to be a great day of intrigue and revelation. We already knew it would be a great lesson when more than one teacher was present, but here were all the classes from all the groups attending this one lecture. Even the creation lecture had not been this momentous.

I stood in formation with my class and the scribe angels filed in and took their various places along the rows. One scribe positioned himself at either end of each row.

They were powerful angels with sharp expressions, always observant and documenting our thoughts and actions with their quick-pens –that's what we called their tools.

These pens would write reams of notes in a flash. The scribing Angels would investigate your mind and pick up all your reactions from what you had been listening to and write them down – and all were recorded in our own books.

Sometimes the scribes, while listening, had blank faces, then they would pick up on something and their expression would light up, or there'd be a flash of bewilderment – but they were superb at hiding their own expressions. We never looked at them as being intrusive. As Angels, we did not mind them been always there. Scribes were always taking notes. It simply was. If they were ever not around, we would feel uncomfortable.

Seymour came and sat down next to me. We were in our comfortable chairs with the rounded arms and joysticks. As Seymour sat down, he grabbed his joystick and fiddled with it like a newcomer.

A scribe angel at the end of our row looked at Seymour and grinned, knowing well that Seymour knew what the gadget was for. Seeing the angel's gaze, realising his silliness had been noted, Seymour released his hand from the joystick and glanced at me a little sheepishly, as if to say, oops, I got caught.

Ralph was in front, giving instructions, with the subordinate teachers forming a long row behind him. Everything was in rank and order, military style. We in the school hall were near the lowest in ranks. Sometimes it was hard to distinguish the higher-ranking angels, because their ranks changed based on the circumstances or tasks. It was these circumstances and tasks that dictated their authority and rank in specific situations. There never was an effort to outdo or outmanoeuvre another member. We all worked in perfect unity and harmony.

"Class 77 to class 84," Ralph began. "Welcome to this great gathering of all the classes – where you will witness a remarkable occurrence. This lesson will teach you about the future of the Kingdom. Man, as we now know him, is from Earth and has everything to gain and to lose just through this one process you will now witness," said Ralph.

"You have all witnessed the creation of man. The whole environment that the Father has placed them into had everything they needed to thrive and enjoy a full life. All of this had worked for the good of man, designed by the Father to become that special close creation that the Father wanted.

But, as you know, man fell from grace and, because of that, the order of things changed. You need to remember – none of this took the Father by surprise.

The Father knew even before he started this process that He would have to manage certain twists and turns in the journey. He knew man would have to suffer and would have to make hard decisions in their lives, but he also knew there would be a victory, a great and mighty victory. A victory that would make even the war worthwhile.

"After man fell, he had to walk in the realm where Satan is prince, and survive under the enemy's rule with little hope for redemption. As part of His victory plan, Father decided that His Son, Jesus, should come down onto the earth, and become man for a season. And in that season, he would be open to all the evil plans of the enemy – plans to tempt Him into sin, including persuading the Son to turn his back on his Father.

"Now even though Jesus was the son of the Father," continued Ralph, "he had to come down to earth and be 100% man. He came with a deep revelation about who He was and a deep understanding of how things were to work. But He had to accomplish in that in a brief season of years, spanning only 33 years, to accomplish the downfall of the enemy.

"Because of what Adam did in the fall, Jesus had to accomplish legally everything that Adam lost. This was a massive sacrifice, as Jesus had to endure much pain and suffering, heartache, disappointment – but He also enjoyed victory. Everything hinged on Jesus legally taking back the authority from the enemy.

"During the life of Jesus in the earthly realm, he tried to teach man about this Kingdom. The teachings went against a lot of what man thought of as normal. Instead of fighting evil with evil, Jesus taught man to fight evil with good. This led to conflict between people in authority, and Jesus. They tried Jesus. You will witness Jesus' trial and the events after the trial – and you will see how all of heaven, our Kingdom, was ordered to stand down and watch. We, at the time of this happening, did not understand the full picture. I have only hinted at it and even while you watch the scenes, you, too, will wonder why the grand army of the Lord did not intervene and wipe out the enemy for good.

"There are many things in this scene that we will go over and we will discuss the intricacies of why things happened the way they did. But, before I give away too much, I want you to sit back and relax and take in everything that you can. The scribes will write down your reactions. We will analyse these at the end and have a great discussion.

"Now, on the right-hand side of your chairs, you will see there is a joystick, and it has a button. As you pull the joystick up, the screen will rise in front of you and will hover in your view. As you look through the screen, you will be taken into the time when this event happened. What you're going to see is the actual event. This is not an act or re-enactment – this is what happened. You will see everybody who was there and what they were doing. By pressing the button on the left-hand side of the joystick, you will see what man sees and see what man shares. You will see the scenes through man's perspective. By releasing the button, you will revert to what you would have seen if you had been present. The scene shifts from a few hundred people to hundreds of thousands of angels when you press the button as the heavenly realms open. When you are ready, we will begin," Ralph concluded.

I looked across at Seymour and he was thumbing the joystick, ready to go. He returned my gaze, looked across at me with a glint in his eye and said, "I've seen this before – this it is something that I can never quite get my head around. I won't spoil it for you Shiloh, but this is enormous."

We all seemed in perfect unity as we pulled back on the joysticks. All our screens flipped up in front of every seat. There were thousands of students watching this programme and, as the screens came up, there was the sound of the screens locking into place in front of us. And then we were suddenly drawn into the blue, watery screen, which seemed to part as we moved straight through a swirling portal and were sucked into the setting of the event. And we all stood around in a courtyard, where the dust was thick, and it was hot.

Everybody was standing around in groups, with headscarves in drab colours wrapped around their heads. Some had sticks in their hands. These staffs seemed common to the gathering – the men would thump them on the ground to emphasise their words. The men and women in the town square were shouting, "Crucify him, crucify that Jesus – he is a heretic."

The roar of the crowd came over the square in, and you could feel their anger in the heat of the day. It was not just any anger: you could feel it dripping with evil that had been influenced by the evil forces. We could see the evil entities jumping onto the people and whispering in their ears. They jumped up and down with ecstatic joy, as their murmurings took hold of the crowd. All were caught up together, shouting. It was awful to witness.

I wanted to shout out, "No, he is innocent!"

We angels stood there, watching from the side-lines, and in the back of my mind I needed to remember that I was still seated in the chair, my hand and the joystick and my finger on the button. I still had my finger firmly pressed down on the right-hand button, so I could see all the realms.

There were thousands upon thousands, upon hundreds of thousands of angels – all lined up, going right up into the sky as far as I could see, surrounding the entire area. It was like a whirlwind of angels, with and all the warrior angels, and all stood in line, in neat rows, and they stood to attention.

CHAPTER 6

They stood with hands gripping their swords, the sun shining on their gloved fists as they clenched and relaxed, the armour making faint sounds with each movement. They were looking with intense glares. All they could see and focus on was their Lord, who was being shouted at and abused.

I caught sight of one group of these warrior angels, who were bowmen. I saw one was staring with his hand on the bow, his arrow already placed in the string, waiting for an order he wished would be given. I looked around and I could see the scribe angels writing, monitoring what the people were thinking and how they were reacting to the situation. Every man was monitored, and records written in their own personal books.

They would bring these books out one day and they would make judgements, using the written words against them with these angelic accounts as evidence of what occurred.

On a platform at the one side of the men in authority – who were called Romans – sat the governor, a well dressed man. He had on a purple robe, with lots of generous golden braiding and golden patterns sewn into his tunic. In his big stone chair, which didn't look comfortable, he leaned forward, his elbow on his knee, and shook his head in dismay. Why would these people want this innocent man to die? And then at that point, I pressed the button to see what the man was seeing.

The angels all disappeared out of the scene and there was the man, watching my Lord Jesus on his hands and knees on the floor. He was being laughed at, shouted at and spat at. As He sat almost in a heap on the stone floor that was dirty, full of dust and hot from the midday sun.

The judgement was passed, and the crowd roared with satisfaction at what was about to happen. I could see the religious rulers of the time – the Pharisees and the Sadducees – these were the religious rulers of the time, rubbing their hands together with glee, for they were as convinced as their oppressors, the Romans, that this man Jesus was a mighty threat to their occupied territory.

They had convinced the Romans that Jesus would entice the locals and the Jewish community to rebel against the Roman Empire.

The governor was not a patient man, even though his wife had been given a dream by God the night before. She had been warned in the dream that her husband, the governor, should let Jesus go.

But the crowd intimidated the governor. He washed his hands of the whole deed and sentenced Jesus to death. As a last attempt to rid himself of any association with the murder of an innocent man, he offered a fellow prisoner instead, who was a convicted murderer. But the crowd grew restless and demanded Jesus' blood. The Governor said, "It is customary to offer a pardon to a Jew on a holiday. So you may choose. Who do you want freed? This convicted murderer, or Jesus?"

The crowd, spurred on by the evil hordes, yelled, "Crucify Jesus!".

The chants rose with anger and hatred. The Governor ceremoniously washed his hands and said,

"Take Jesus to be crucified."

At the sound of this, the crowd roared with victory.

I pressed the button to show the real sounds, and I saw Satan and all his hordes jumping up and down in absolute joy, which I have never, in all the lessons I had been in, seen before – the evil ones were somersaulting and dancing with joy. At long last they had got their enemy, their ultimate enemy. They were going to destroy Jesus and the Father would have to pay the ultimate price. The Father would lose his only son.

The enemy hordes energetically jumped, shouted, and laughed, fuelling negative thoughts and intensifying hatred. There was such an overpowering sense of evil, it was almost putrid smelling, so vile that I .... I couldn't understand how man could not sense it. It hung so thickly in the air! It was so prevalent, so obvious.

They took Jesus to a portion of the square where they tied Him up against a post and they removed his cloak. His bare back was dripping with sweat from the heat of the day.

A Roman soldier moved forward. He had lots of badges and emblems on top of his hardened leather breastplate. He was a man of high rank, and he commanded another man of lesser rank to give Jesus the whip.

"Let the whipping begin!" he shouted, "but do not whip him over 39 times, for this is the law. He is not a Roman citizen and may only be beaten 39 times. But give him the maximum."

This he did in order that the crowd would not ask for more and would be satisfied with this terrible punishment that he had now ordered. The other, lowly soldier stepped forward with a long leather whip in his hand. It divided after a few feet into nine strands. There were bits of metal and bone tied to the ends of each strand. This whip cruelly ripped the flesh off a man's back, inflicting extensive damage to the skin and muscle, without killing the victim. The crowd was waiting with anticipation for the pain. This was something I could not understand at all. Why did they take such enjoyment out of seeing pain and suffering in one of their own kind? It made no sense to any of us.

Down came the first stroke, with a swish through the air, the crowd hushed in anticipation. Even the breath of Jesus halted. The strands wrapped themselves around the side of his rib cage and the ends of the bones and the pieces of metal dug deep into the skin, right down to the bone. I could hear the slashing of the whip as the hooks gripped into the flesh of the body. Then the soldier pulled the whip violently back and, as it came loose from the body, it ripped part of the flesh off, which he took off and flung it behind his shoulder, readying the torture instrument for the next whipping. In this way, bits of flesh were flung into the air and blood splattered everywhere.

The commander shouted, "One!"

The soldier played with the whip, almost tormenting Jesus by prolonging the next 38 strokes. Then he untangled the whip and brought it down again. The edges came around and gripped onto Jesus' stomach this time, digging in deep. The sound of the whip hitting the flesh, which was now wet from the dripping blood, made a slapping sound and Jesus groaned in pain. The soldier gleefully pulled the whip back and ripped open Jesus' stomach.

The commander shouted, "Two!"

This continued for some time: three, four, five. The blood had poured itself onto the floor of the square and Jesus slipped onto his knees, his hands held above his head, down to the round metal clasp that held him tied to the post. With every stroke that Jesus received, the entire army of the Lord lifted the blades of their swords by the hilts' thumb links – and then shoved them back down again. I heard the resounding clicks and then a sliding sound as the metal came slightly out under the hilt, and then a chump sound, as thousands of swords re-seated themselves simultaneously, with the clicking back into the scabbards. They all seemed to lean in unison as they clicked the hungry blades back, wanting with every bit of their existence to destroy the enemy. But they had been given strict orders from the King, from our Father, not to intervene, but only to watch, to be witnesses only, never to break rank, no matter what happened. They were only there to witness this significant event.

The scribes were recording every single bloody stripe that Jesus received and at the top of the page they wrote, in bold letters, the victorious statement. The scribe next to me tilted his book so that I could see what he was writing, and there, on top of each note in capital letters, were mighty words of victory, as follows. –

Stroke one, sickness of the bones.

Stroke two, blood disorders.

Stroke three, tumorous growth and cancer.

Stroke four ...

The list went on for every stroke that the whip tore into his flesh. Jesus won a monumental victory for the men and women that made him endure such suffering. I pressed the left button twice on the joystick and up came a scroll of evidence and writings that were in the book that the Father had given for man to rule in victory. His love for them had been foretold by the prophets in that wonderful book that the Jews had held so close to the hearts. Just as in the books written by Moses, they claimed that no sinner in the Jewish culture should be struck over 40 times for being a sinner. That was why Pilate felt he needed to follow the Jewish tradition more than the Roman one, as Jesus was not a Roman. Flogging a man before crucifixion was just an evil and horrible punishment by torture, as it inflicted such immense pain in the body, without killing the man.

In the book of the Torah, the prophet Isaiah prophesied this very thing would happen to the son of God, and he said that he would be wounded for the transgressions of man, and would be bruised for their iniquities and that the chastisement of man's peace would be upon him.

"And with his stripes man would be healed."

I saw events unfolding on the main screen and understood what was happening.

The stripes I witnessed were a means of healing for humanity. That was part of the victory that we had heard about. Each lash inspired the scribes to write victorious headlines about man's freedom from sicknesses, diseases, and infirmities. Through the Blood that was shed, Jesus won everything back from the enemy.

The enemy was unaware of what was happening. They just saw only their temporary victory. They were killing and hurting the beloved Son of the most high God. But our Father God was busy legally winning.

The commentary from the consul in front of us was giving a rundown of the background of the situation we were witnessing.

Ralph interjected and told the classes,

"Jesus even said to his followers a few days before this event that He is like the good Shepherd who looks after his sheep and would protect the sheep at all costs – even if it cost the shepherd's life. He continued to tell His followers that He knew who He was, just as the Father knew Him.

"He knew the Father, and was ready to lay down his life for the sheep that He cared for and loved so much. And for that reason, the Father, in return, loved unconditionally because He would lay down His life for the ones that the Father loved so much."

"And then He laid down his life through his own will, as you are witnessing. He chose this path, and that He had the authority to rise again to be with the Father.

"He said this to all His followers, yet they did not understand what Jesus was saying until after this terrible event. Jesus knew what he was doing and what He had to suffer in order to accomplish what the Father wanted, and he did it because He loved those people that hurt Him so much."

The power of love was probably the greatest lesson we had to learn as angels. We angels couldn't help but love the Father unconditionally, but man had a choice in whether or not to love the Father.

It was hard for us angels to understand this, after knowing everything the Father had done. After everything He created, after all man had done in return. Man had rejected the Father and rather settled for temporary rewards from the evil ones, as opposed to eternal victory with the Father.

Jesus still went through all this pain and suffering, even though he knew man would react in a selfish and temporal way. But Jesus knew that one day the human soul would have the opportunity to get back to our kingdom in heaven.

When the lashing stopped, the Roman soldier was out of breath and he was convinced he had not gone over the said limit, so he dropped the whip and looked in dismay at the crumpled form of a human being, lying in the pool of blood and flesh.

The soldier's conscience was perturbed by what lay before him. The excuse he mustered was that he had only been following orders. But this, he knew deep down, was not valid, and he was as guilty as the governor for inflicting such pain and suffering on Jesus.

This did not stop the other soldiers from laughing and jeering and spitting on Jesus. Another soldier made a crown out of thorn branches and put it on Jesus' head, mocking him as the "King of the Jews."

They tied Jesus' hands to the crossbeam of the cross he would be nailed to and told him to carry it up the hill. Jesus had to walk, but he could barely keep himself upright. He struggled up the hill, carrying more than just the cross as His burden. Every angel watching leaned forward, with their hearts fighting the ingrained discipline to intervene – either by carrying their beloved Jesus and the beam to its final destination, or to immolate the enemy and save their master and Lord, but the order was given again,

"Easy, stand fast. That's an order!"

A man in the crowd came out to help and gave water to Jesus to drink. He had been one of Jesus' followers and was instructed by the Roman soldiers, whose bloodthirst had diminished somewhat, what with all the lashings, and they just were keen to end this day. So they ordered the man to carry the beam up the hill for Jesus and this he did.

When they arrived at the top of the hill, there were two other crosses already up. The soldiers ordered everyone to move back, so they could make space around the base of the hole that had already been dug in the ground. There were people milling around, some laughing and some sobbing, a mixture of utter hatred and heartbreak.

Jesus was forced onto the ground on his back, and they put the beam underneath His shoulders. They stretched out His arms and two burly soldiers held them down. Jesus was looking up heaven, and it seemed as if He was looking at us. Another soldier offered a spike and nailed it into His wrist, fixing His left hand. Then, ignoring the gurgling scream, he smashed the other spike into the right wrist, fixing both hands to the beam. Once His hands were fixed, they pulled Jesus up, and the beam placed on top of a upright and fixed in place. Then his feet were crossed over at the ankles and they put a single spike through both feet, just above the ankles and into the wood. Three soldiers stepped forward and, with practised precision, lifted the cross and slid the brace into the gaping hole. The cross slid in and was pushed upright, all in a single smooth movement, ending with a sudden jolt, as the cross settled into its position. A shivering sound went through all the ranks of the angels as they watched their beloved Jesus, the leader of our army, being pinned to this wooden cross.

Jesus knew what was happening, even though Satan and his hordes thought they had the victory and that they had won and, at long last, had defeated the Father. The by-standers and soldiers mocked Jesus on the cross, laughing and jeering at his torn, naked flesh. They even gambled over his clothes.

His closest disciples and his mother Mary were in the crowd, witnessing this whole procedure. We watched the crowd, still enthused by the blood-letting, shout abuse at the now limp body. The world seemed to groan as the sky grew dark, blocking out the sun. A thick gloom descended, and the air even felt heavy. Many had seen nothing like this before. The ground shook, and the cross seemed to dance in the dim light. There was a deep rumbling, and an earthquake shook the ground for miles around. That was when Jesus raised his head and shouted out to the Father in despair.

"My God, my God, why have you forsaken me?"

CHAPTER 6

That was the moment in which Jesus took all the sin of the world on himself, and even the Father had to turn away from his Son, as He could not look upon all that sin. This is when Jesus died to accomplish his divine task, known only by the Godhead.

We would need Ralph to explain to us angels later, because even as we watched, it didn't make sense. I pressed the button on the joystick and could see men and women crying in anguish at the foot of the cross. The soldiers were uninterested, and the bystanders looked confused. I pressed the joystick controls again and noticed that the enemy, too, was focused on their victory. They called a group of entities of various shapes and sizes, known as the intimidators, to come down to the pit, which was their home, and celebrate their triumph. We saw them leave, peel themselves off the men and women, and slither into the ground. Soon, all had gone. The warrior angels stood to attention in silence, their hands gloved firmly on their hilts, and waited for the command that never came.

The Roman soldier came forward and said, "Are they dead yet?"

A few young soldiers stepped forward and looked up into the face of the of the one thief on the right of our Lord and saw he was still breathing. The second took a hammer, large and brutal –looking, and smashed the legs of the man. The man now could not lift his body up in order to breathe and slumped down and slowly gurgled his last breath as he died.

The soldier went on to the Lord and looked up and saw he was dead already. The second soldier raised the hammer, but the senior soldier lifted his arm up to stop him and said, "Wait, use the spear and piece his side to make sure."

The junior soldier lifted the spear and thrust it into our Lord's side. All the angels shuddered and seemed to feel that spear pierce deep into their sides. Blood and water came out as the blood was separating from itself and clotting into water and blood clots. That was a sure sign the heart had stopped and the man would be dead.

The soldiers nodded at each other, not needing any further intervention, and then went and smashed the other thief's legs and he groaned and died, slumped over.

All went quiet except, of course, for the sobbing of the women at the base of the cross.

The sky opened up again as the crowd moved away. Many of the people were wondering what had just happened. Why had they been so riled up to kill such an amazing, gentle and loving man who had done no one any harm? All he had ever done was to help people get better and teach bold words of truth. Surely he had been special, yet they had hounded him to his death. Most hung their heads in dismay and were perplexed why they had acted so cold-heartedly towards someone they had admired and cheered only a few days before.

One woman at the feet of Jesus said to the commanding officer,

"Sir, we have a grave for our Lord. Can we please take him there, as the day is drawing to a close and it would be good to get him cleaned and buried as the law requires?"

"Yes, alright," replied the officer and told his soldiers to take the cross down and hand Jesus over.

We watched as the limp, lifeless body was placed on the ground and was taken off to the allocated grave.

We all sat silently in our encompassing chairs. Even the chairs seemed to be moved to silence.

Ralph stood up slowly and said, "Now you all have witnessed the greatest battle of this war. Because of this victory, everything the enemy has done is pointless and has no substance. Our Lord was victorious. It will be shown to you in another lesson that He took the keys from the enemy, giving you a taster of the many victorious lessons you will yet see.

Bang, bang went the shields of the warrior angels, who were still present, and up they went in perfect formation. The large, magnificent angel Michael stepped forward and smiled at me and nodded.

"You, Master Shiloh, will enjoy the next lesson."

He bowed his head in an informal salute, winked at Ralph and then disappeared.

Seymour stared in my direction.

"I have known Michael forever, and he has never said that to me," he blurted in amazement.

With that, the day's first lesson was closed. We all lingered in our seats, pondering over what we had witnessed.

Chapter 7

The Corruption of Man's Bloodline

The next day, I surveyed the expansive hall filled with rows of desks and occupied seats as I contemplated what we had witnessed the previous day. Most of the students were in the same deep-thinking mode as I. We had seen Jesus, the Son, sacrificing himself for all of humanity. Despite having the choice to withdraw, He prioritised the future of humanity. Christ, the Son of God, had willingly given his life to atone for the sins of humankind. Despite having the option to abandon humanity to their fallen nature, Jesus had instead chosen to secure the future salvation of all people. His selfless act had resonated profoundly with us all. Ralph interrupted our thoughts.

"Yesterday, you were presented with much information that you couldn't fully comprehend, but I'll do my best to help you understand some of it," Ralph said. "Jesus gave humanity the authority over man's realm again by taking on the fall of man and defeating Satan's authority.

"In today's lesson, we will see what happened next. Remember, Jesus is with us and has triumphed in the battle. He has reclaimed all authority from the fallen one and entrusted it to humanity. It's up to you now to assist man in understanding and embracing this authority, and help lead him to a satisfying life.

"So, today you will once more visit the realm of man, and witness more deception by the fallen ones. These fallen angels want to be like the Father, but as the Father created them, the entities have their limitations. They desire to be worshipped and want to be gods in their realm. Their subjects of choice are humanity. The one sure-found flaw of humanity since the fall is man's desire to have power over any competition from his kind, any animal or even plants. Now observe," instructed Ralph.

The screens appeared before us and we looked at the deception unravelling. There stood the fallen one – he was huge and had powerful arms with broad hands. His eyes were murky with an intensity that we could not endure.

The fallen angel cut an imposing figure, standing taller and stronger than any mortal, with a threatening sneer across his face. Dark, spiked armour stressed his muscular frame. In his grip was a heavy spear, gripped tight in hands that could crush a man's skull. Smooth ebony wings had once extended from his back, now they were tattered and stained grey, having been cast from heaven. The glory of the heavenly realm was lacking in this earthly realm and, despite his imposing presence, seemed to have taken its toll.

This sinister being strode across the land, believing himself superior to all humans. In his pride, he craved the obedience and reverence rightfully belonging to the Creator. He aspired to rule over humanity as a god, using deceit and intimidation to corrupt the weak-willed. The fallen angel underestimated the resolve of mankind, he was confident they would submit to his will and authority.

Ralph commented, "Yet his formidable power is finite, while humanity's potential is infinite. People need only find the truth to see through his lies. Those who turn toward wisdom and justice would recognise every being has a choice – even when that choice seems difficult. And with perseverance, they will understand sacrifice and love can overcome any evil, if only they dare to try. The fallen angel might be terrifying, but he does not own the souls of men. That power still resides within each individual, once they claim it as their own."

The fallen angel paced, his spiked armour clinking with each thudding step. Grimy, yet glinting in the firelight, the links of chain mail betrayed countless violent deeds. But now we noticed that he was not there to flaunt his power this time. No, the fallen one had come to negotiate.

Into the gloomy chamber, in which the fallen angel had been pacing to and fro, strode a worldly human king, draped in soft red robes lined with white fur. Though he bore a golden crown atop his head, the regal man paled, compared to the towering fallen angel glowering down at him.

The king did his best to hide the unease churning within. He had convinced himself what he was about to do was necessary for the good of the kingdom. But now, facing the monstrous fallen angel and the cruel bargain they had struck, doubt began creeping into his mind. Could he trade his daughter for promises of power from this sinister being?

"Well?" the angel snarled, fists clenching his spear in anticipation. "Have you brought her or not?"

The king swallowed hard, suppressing his misgivings before giving a nod.

"Yes ... the deal is intact. My daughter awaits you."

He turned and swept a hand toward the chamber entrance.

The angel tossed a manuscript from under his rough garment. It seemed to glide with ease towards the king. The king reached out to take it, but it remained in mid-flight and unrolled itself.

It was alive. On the scroll were designs and handwriting. They moved around the scroll impulsively.

"King, you don't get to read the concealed messages without first presenting me with my price. If I am contented, then the words and diagrams will obey your wish to have powerful knowledge."

As we observed the scene from our console chairs, our hands gripped the joysticks and our fingers hovered over the buttons, that, when pressed, would reveal more depth to what we could see. Ralph instructed us to investigate the mind of the king. The scene changed to another level, and we saw the king's mind seemed to waver and be open to our intrusion.

"Look into the king's mind, class, and try to understand his motive," said Ralph. "See why he will let this creature defile his daughter? What does he hope to gain?"

We pressed the button more tentatively, as we anticipated another level of man's mind that we were unfamiliar with.

We looked at the king's head and then dived into his mind. Light and waves swirled. Then I heard a voice.

"Now I can defeat my brother and destroy him for all time, and I will eradicate him from all memory. He will at long last be defeated. Oh my, I can have all his land and even his wives. As for his children, I will offer them up to my new god."

His deep hate and anger and jealousy smelled sour. The smell of a rotten corpse rose into my nostrils.

"Urgh!" I said and pulled myself out and back to myself.

Ralph looked at me and said, "Can't you stand it, Shiloh? You need to understand what drives man. He does not see things as you do, but is ambitious for self-gain. This is confusing, but the enemy uses it to gain strongholds."

"How can man prevent this?" I inquired.

"Well, he needs to become more selfless, not always thinking about himself."

"Now, watch what the monarch does," he directed my attention back to the king.

"Lord, what do you hope to attain by having my daughter?" demanded the king.

"Ha, now you dwindle and show concern," smirked the angel. "Only a short while ago, all you wanted was the secret parchment and, of course, the power and authority it will give you," he reminded the king. "Yes, I know about your brother, who wants his throne back, and the elite army he has assembled in the north. He is waiting for the springtime when he will march his infantry across the plains, where he will confront you and slaughter you. "What I plan with your daughter has a much greater value and destiny than either you or your brother," the angel said imperiously, adding, "But that is not your concern. Your only concern is to honour our arrangement."

There was a loud banging on the solid oak door of the main hall. The thump echoed through the stone passage to where we watched from. From our console chairs, we could change our viewpoint and with a flip of the button on our joystick, we were looking at the monarchs from the balcony. The balcony surrounded the great hall of the king's chamber. It had a wooden floor and even creaked and made hollow thumps as the joystick followed all the way along the narrow balcony, making it all real and intense. I even felt my chair vibrate. The total experience from the console chair was immersive and helped us grasp the different perspectives of what we were observing. We could transverse anywhere in the room, but the balcony gave a wonderful angle, we were close by, but felt safe. From our elevated position, we could also hear the conversations that took place.

In came the daughter, flanked by four armed guards.

"Sir, your daughter, as you requested," said the leader of the group.

"Thank you, Manfred," said the king, and motioned to his daughter to approach his side.

The angel had his back to her. She whispered, "Who is he, father?"

"This, my dear, is going to be your husband; he is a powerful lord, who desires you to be his ... wife," said the king.

"But, father, this is forbidden. He is not of pure blood. My children will not inherit your kingdom," protested the daughter.

CHAPTER 7

The angel turned. "So, you have opinions and a mind. You might consider that my kingdom is even more attractive than a human one. Am I not the lord of your kingdom too? Will this not mean you will be queen over far much more?"

He looked into her eyes and waited for the correct response.

"I suppose you are correct, my lord. I should not question you and your status, as I am merely the daughter of the king, my lord," she replied, with a fearful glance at her father the king.

"Good, then all is settled. I will show you a new world after you leave with me. We will please my kingdom until judgement day comes." The fallen angel laughed coldly. "You have done well, mortal king. Our contract is complete."

He grabbed the daughter of the king harshly, overpowering any resistance. The king watched as his daughter was taken, a profound shame and sorrow filling him. He had given up his authority as a father and ruler. Could his people's faith help reclaim what he had surrendered?

The angel wrapped his cloak around her and vanished, leaving the parchment to float to the cold stone floor at the feet of the king. The words and diagrams returned to the page and set themselves in order.

The head guard tried to grab the scroll, but the king stopped him. He reached down and swooped up the scroll and clutched it to his breast.

Turning to the guards, he instructed them to tell no one what they had seen, adding that he would reward them for their loyalty.

With that, they bowed and left the king's hall.

The king walked over to his throne. Seymour and I dived into his mind again. We looked deep into its recesses. The sacrifice of his daughter troubled him, he knew he had put her life in danger and that he had broken the sacred rule.

"Never cross that line," he heard his father's voice warning him, "My son, you will need to carry much, but never cross the line of giving your bloodline to the fallen lords, they only have their own good at heart. You cannot conquer their treachery. It is bigger than our kingdom. Promise me, son, you will never fall for their wicked plans."

Then we saw him defend himself from a guilty conscience, using his greed and fear to pushed the oath aside and saying to himself, "Times are not the same as they were for my father. If I don't do this, I'll die and my entire kingdom with me. I have nothing else but to pursue this, and I have a lot to gain."

The putrid smell swirled around his mind, and now there was a red thick cloud. Seymour and I left the king's consciousness and returned to the class.

"So, what did you see?" asked Cosmos.

"Humans have a way of convincing themselves that as long as they are secure and d the way they want to be, then anything is ok," answered Seymour.

Ralph commented, "Good answer, Seymour. Yes, man is not like us, and that fallen one knows it. See how he uses his words to seduce and comfort the man? He knows what the man is thinking in his mind.

"Man will be haunted from the beginning of the great deception until the end. The fallen angel believes that corrupting man's bloodline will cause a change to the genetic code set by the Father. The genetic code has many properties. The physical ones in the code are embedded instructions to the cells on how they will grow and develop, determining characteristics of skin and hair colour, of the height and build of the man, and attributes like how his mind will think and how he will behave. But they shared these attributes between the mother and father of the offspring, and the offspring inherits half from his dad and half from his mother.

"That is why, once corruption enters the line, it will be passed on. You are not formed by two, your Father alone formed you. And you are not the same as man, even if some of us resemble man. Not you, of course, Seymour," he chuckled with a wink.

"Genetic coding is precise," he went on, "and, when breached or changed, the corruption will multiply and increase. The angel knows the plan of the Father to have each man's soul return to the Father, but there are two conditions the Father has set out that make it pure. One is that man must have free will to choose to return home or not. Second, he must not have corrupted genes. The angel knows this, and he plans to corrupt the bloodline of this king. The offspring will devastate mankind. This king has not heeded his father's wisdom and will regret his fearful decision."

This king has not listened to his father's advice and will regret his choice. And it will affect more than just his reign, but the entire kingdom. That's what happens when you don't listen to the wisdom of those who have gone before. The king's decision will have far-reaching consequences. He will learn the hard way what it means to lead and to listen to those who have gone before.

The consequences of his mistake will make sure that future kings remember to listen to what their ancestors have to say, and to think of more than just themselves. This story will be passed down for years to come as a reminder of what can go wrong when a young man believes he knows better than those who came before him. These gods or fallen angels, with their vast reservoirs of ancient knowledge, possess secrets that mortal men can scarcely comprehend. Of course, mankind yearns for such enlightenment, driven by an insatiable thirst for power and understanding.

Yet the toll demanded for this prohibited wisdom is exorbitant - as in reaching for celestial understanding, humans unknowingly craft the very shackles of their own captivity. By embracing the offerings of these semi-divine entities, mortals discover themselves tethered in servitude, their autonomy gradually eroded by the very creatures from whom they sought enlightenment.

* * *

Now, many of you guardians must be wondering why the more powerful fallen angels are so eager to interbreed with mere human mortals. There is a compelling reason behind this desire. The fallen ones do not actually possess the authority to rule over mankind, even though humans have lost much of their own authority due to the Fall. In order for the fallen ones to establish a power structure that is regarded as legitimate, they must somehow utilize the bloodline of kings.

Their strategy involves taking human women as wives and using the offspring of these unions to become the future rulers of the earthly realm. These hybrid children are known as Nephilim. Because the Nephilim closely resemble humans in appearance while possessing extraordinary powers and knowledge beyond mortal capabilities, they will be more readily accepted as legal and rightful rulers by the general population.

This calculated plan allows the fallen angels to indirectly exert control over humanity through their powerful offspring, circumventing their lack of direct authority. The Nephilim serve as a bridge between the celestial and mortal worlds, combining the strengths of both while masking their true origins from unsuspecting humans.

Now I'm sure you want to see a true example of this fascinating phenomenon, so I will direct your attention to file 74 on the control panel. This particular file contains a riveting account of a pivotal event in which a young boy is confronted by a formidable Nephilim. The encounter is nothing short of extraordinary, as the Nephilim stands at an imposing height of 11 feet and possesses tremendous strength. In stark contrast, the boy, named David, is a mere wisp of a child, standing just a bit over 5 feet tall and only eleven years of age. This dramatic disparity in size and power sets the stage for an unforgettable clash between mortal and hybrid, showcasing the awe-inspiring capabilities of these celestial-human offspring.

Shiloh, with eager anticipation, was the first to reach out and locate file 74. Without hesitation, he launched himself into the story, his essence merging with the digital narrative. Seymour, ever the supportive mentor, followed closely behind, ready to guide and observe.

As the file whirred to life, Shiloh found himself transported to the dusty, sun-baked plain of the battlefield. He was surrounded by rolling hills, upon which a massive army stood, their voices raised in a cacophony of chants and shouts. The clashing of heavy bronze shields and the ringing of swords thundered across the plain, echoing off the nearby slopes. On the opposing hill, in stark contrast, stood the army of King Saul. Their silence was palpable, a stark testament to the fear that gripped their hearts. The prospect of becoming slaves to the Philistines had left them disheartened and paralyzed.

Suddenly, a few seconds behind the eager apprentice, with a familiar thwack, Seymour materialized next to Shiloh. A knowing grin spread across his face as he turned to his young protégé. "I know this scene in intricate detail," he said, his voice tinged with excitement and nostalgia. "Ralph brought me here as an apprentice, and it was the real thing – not just a simulation. Now, watch closely. You're about to witness how the courage of a boy can overpower even the mightiest of giants."

Now class," said the all-too-familiar voice of Ralph, who had materialized to the left, accompanied by the rest of Class 84. His ancient eyes sparkled with wisdom as he addressed the young angels. "What you're about to witness is a true depiction of courage and a young boy's unwavering understanding and faith in our Father God. He knows, deep in his heart, that the Father will protect him. All he possesses is his boundless courage and that simple slingshot, along with the five smooth stones he carefully selected from the riverbed."

Ralph paused, allowing his words to sink in before continuing, "Now, you might be wondering why David chose five stones. Did he doubt his aim? Oh no, my dear students. David knew full well that Goliath had brothers, and in his resolute spirit, he intended to vanquish them too if necessary."

The assembled angels fell into a quiet stillness as they observed the events unfolding in front of them, taking in every aspect of that momentous valley with their otherworldly perceptions. The atmosphere was heavy with dust, carrying the strong smell of men and their anxiety. The intense heat of the day pressed down on the land, heightening the suspense that lingered in the air like a weighty garment. Every angel remained captivated, their celestial shapes completely motionless as they observed this crucial juncture in human history.

Ralph instructed the class about a button on the console that he had activated, which would produce a printout of the current situation. With a sweeping gesture, he distributed rolled-up scrolls to each student. Shiloh reached out and the scroll sunk into his hand. Revealing the contents of the scroll.

The Field of Battle: Valleys and Suspense

The story unfolds in the Vale of Elah, a breathtaking yet foreboding landscape. Two conflicting armies, the Israelites and the Philistines, have established their camps on opposing slopes, with the valley spreading out between them. This valley serves as the backdrop for what will become one of the most renowned clashes in history. The harsh daylight beats down upon the craggy terrain, while sparse plant life hints at the unforgiving environment. The valley seems filled with a heavy, oppressive tension, as if time itself is holding its breath.

King Saul: Paralyzed by Fear

Saul, the commander of the Israelite forces, is in a difficult situation. Formerly a formidable fighter, Saul now trembles under the heavy burden of dread. Goliath, the colossal Philistine, has been provoking the Israelites for forty days—every day approaching and mocking them, calling for a champion to engage in single combat. Despite being a king, and a large man himself said to be chosen as king because he was head and shoulders above other men. Saul senses his bravery diminishing with each insult, incapable of stepping up to confront the monstrous Goliath.

Goliath: The Titan of Terror

Goliath is a colossus of a man, standing over nine feet tall. His towering figure is sheathed in bronze armor, reflecting the harsh sunlight, and making him appear almost invincible. His helmet, breastplate, and greaves gleam ominously, and his javelin and spear are imposing, with the spearhead alone weighing about fifteen pounds. His shield-bearer walks ahead of him, adding to the intimidation. Goliath's voice booms across the valley as he hurls insults and challenges, further demoralizing the Israelite forces.

David: The Unlikely Hero

In stark contrast, David is a young shepherd boy, not even a warrior. He arrives at the battlefield bringing provisions for his older brothers who serve in Saul's army. Upon hearing Goliath's taunts, David's righteous indignation flares. Unlike the seasoned soldiers around him, David is undeterred by Goliath's size and bravado. His faith in God's deliverance is unshakeable. Dressed in simple shepherd's garb, with no armor to encumber him, David's only weapon is a sling and five smooth stones he gathers from a nearby brook.

The Confrontation: Faith vs. Fury

Goliath laughs at David's approach, his disdain and scorn evident. The giant's voice carries across the battlefield, causing many of the Israelite soldiers to flinch. "Am I a dog, that you come at me with sticks?" he shouts, clearly not impressed. He narrows his eyes at the young shepherd, but David does not waver. He stands straight and looks Goliath in the eye. "You come against me with sword and spear and javelin, but I come against you in the name of the LORD Almighty, the God of the armies of Israel, whom you have defied," he says loud enough for the whole valley to hear.

As the two draw closer, the sheer disparity becomes clear—size against skill, brute strength against precision. Goliath towers over David, his shadow engulfing the young shepherd. The Philistine's armor gleams in the sunlight, a stark contrast to David's simple tunic. Onlookers hold their breath, many fearing for the boy's life. With practiced movements, David reaches into his pouch and selects a smooth stone. He fits it into his sling, the leather worn and familiar in his hands. Whirling it with practiced ease, the sling becomes a blur of motion. The tension mounts as David takes aim, his muscles coiled like a spring. With a decisive release, the stone hurtles through the air, a barely visible projectile. It strikes Goliath squarely on the forehead with a sickening crack, finding the one vulnerable spot in his imposing armor. The impact is immediate and devastating; Goliath's eyes roll back, and his mighty form sways for a moment before crashing to the ground with a thunderous echo that seems to shake the very earth. A stunned silence falls over the battlefield as dust settles around the fallen giant.

Victory and Shock

The Philistine ranks break into chaos and retreat as disbelief spreads through their lines. The Israelites, rejuvenated by this miraculous victory, charge forward, routing the fleeing Philistines. David stands over the fallen Goliath, taking the giant's own sword to decapitate him, ensuring that there would be no doubt about the outcome.

"This epic showdown between David and Goliath is a timeless testament to faith and courage, contrasting the volatile ferocity of Goliath with the unwavering faith and skill of young David. The battlefield of the Valley of Elah, with its imposing natural amphitheater, serves as the perfect setting for this legendary confrontation." said Ralph.

Shiloh had the story firmly etched in his mind after poring over the ancient scroll, but nothing could have prepared him for the visceral reality unfolding before his eyes. Here

CHAPTER 7

he was, standing amidst the swirling dust and spilled blood, bearing witness to the giant's dramatic downfall. The clash of metal, the cries of soldiers, and the acrid scent of battle filled his senses, bringing the legendary tale to life in a way no written word ever could. As he watched David triumph over Goliath, Shiloh felt a surge of awe and understanding realizing that some stories could only truly be grasped when experienced firsthand.

Shiloh stood riveted, the vibrant energy of the scene washing over him. He watched as David, chest heaving with adrenaline, gripped the giant's sword in both hands, a symbol of triumph and defiance.

"Look at that!" Seymour exclaimed, his voice a mix of awe and pride. "That boy is about to change everything."

Ralph nodded solemnly, eyes glinting with wisdom. "David understands that true strength comes not from size but from faith."

The young angels leaned closer, entranced by the raw power of the moment. The atmosphere crackled with excitement as they witnessed the impact of David's victory ripple through both armies.

As the dust settled around Goliath's lifeless form, murmurs began to stir among the Israelite soldiers. Their faces shifted from shock to disbelief, then blossomed into unrestrained joy.

"David! David!" they chanted, voices rising like a tidal wave. The sound echoed off the valley walls, reverberating in Shiloh's chest.

The boy's shoulders straightened at their cries. With each shout of his name, he seemed to grow taller, more radiant. He lifted Goliath's severed head high above him; blood trickled down his arm as he brandished it like a trophy.

"Look at them!" Shiloh pointed toward King Saul's camp, where faces turned from despair to hope.

Seymour grinned wide. "Now they know they can stand against fear!"

David turned toward King Saul's army, their morale swelling like a rising tide. His youthful face glowed with fierce determination and an unshakeable faith in God.

"What do you see?" Ralph asked, nudging Shiloh gently to engage his focus.

Shiloh took a breath and observed closely. "They believe now," he replied softly. "David showed them what faith can do."

Ralph smiled approvingly, his ancient eyes glinting with a mixture of pride and anticipation. He raised a hand, motioning for everyone to gather around and watch closely as King Saul, the towering figure draped in regal attire, approached David with a determined stride. The mood hung heavy and electric, pregnant with the certainty that destiny stood poised to shift.

Shiloh could sense that the King felt ashamed of his lack of courage, while a young shepherd had accomplished what he ought to have. This also sparked a jealousy of the Father's favor on David.

As King Saul approached, the army fell silent, eyes darting between the young boy and their leader. The weight of the moment hung heavy in the air. David, still clutching Goliath's severed head, stood firm, chest rising and falling with each breath.

Saul's gaze bore into David, a mixture of astonishment and uncertainty swirling in his eyes. "Who are you?" he asked, voice steady yet tinged with disbelief.

"David," the boy replied, his voice ringing clear across the valley. "Son of Jesse."

A murmur rippled through the ranks of soldiers as they processed the name. This was no warrior but a mere shepherd boy who had dared to face a giant.

"You fought without my armor," Saul noted, skepticism creeping into his tone. "With only a sling and stones?"

David nodded, unfazed by the king's probing gaze. "I didn't come against him for glory or riches but in the name of the LORD Almighty." His voice resonated with conviction, echoing off the hills surrounding them.

The soldiers exchanged glances; awe mixed with respect painted their faces as they recognized that something greater than mere chance had unfolded before them.

Seymour leaned closer to Shiloh, excitement gleaming in his eyes. "See how David speaks? His faith alone transforms him into a mighty warrior."

Ralph nodded appreciatively. "Yes, it is faith that gives strength beyond what seems possible."

Saul's expression shifted from skepticism to contemplation. He studied David's unwavering stance—there was something remarkable about this boy who had stepped up when no one else would.

"Come," Saul finally said, extending a hand toward David. "You will be rewarded for this great victory."

David lowered Goliath's head slowly the head of the giant settled into the dust with a soft squishing sound yet, David remained steadfast where he stood before the monarch.

"Reward? I seek not gold nor title," David replied firmly. "My heart beats for my people and our God."

CHAPTER 7

The air buzzed with anticipation as Saul regarded him with newfound respect—a king humbled by a boy's conviction.

Around them, cheers erupted as soldiers rallied behind David's defiance of fear and despair. They began chanting his name again: "David! David!"

Ralph smiled softly at Shiloh while nodding toward their surroundings. "This is how courage inspires others."

Shiloh took it all in—the transformation in both David and Saul—and felt hope swell within him like an unquenchable fire igniting every corner of his spirit.

Seymour squeezed Shiloh's shoulder gently as they watched history unfold before them—an indelible moment carved into time that would echo for generations to come...

The King's forehead creased as he observed David's determination. Tension filled the space between them as everyone waited for Saul's next utterance.

The moment lingered, vibrant with energy and excitement as their discussion started to unravel against the backdrop of renewed hope and bravery reverberating through the valley.

Ralph remarked that they would now have vanquished the enemy of God's people in a manner that brings glory to God the Father, not to an earthly king or man.

The students gathered in the sprawling valley, the earth saturated with the blood of the giant. Ralph proclaimed, "Now, students, the giant is a manifestation of the enemy's attempt to alter the human gene pool. However, the lineage formed by the mortal kings and the fallen angels persists, and as we progress through the eras of humanity, you will see the turmoil this lineage has stirred in human history."

Ralph's words hung heavy in the air as the young angels absorbed the gravity of his statement. Shiloh felt a shiver run through his celestial form, realizing the depth of the battle they were witnessing extended far beyond this single confrontation.

"But sir," one of the other students piped up, his voice tinged with confusion, "how can a lineage of fallen angels continue to affect humanity?"

Ralph turned to address the group; his eyes gleaming with wisdom. "Ah, excellent question. You see, the influence of these beings stretches across time like tendrils of darkness. Their offspring, though mortal, carry within them a seed of rebellion against the divine order."

Seymour nodded gravely. "It's not just about physical strength or size," he added. "It's about the corruption of hearts and minds."

As if on cue, the scene before them shifted. The victorious Israelites began to gather the spoils of war, their faces a mixture of joy and greed. Some cast furtive glances at David, envy creeping into their expressions.

Shiloh watched intently as King Saul's demeanor subtly changed. The initial awe in his eyes gave way to a flicker of something darker – jealousy, perhaps, or fear of being overshadowed.

"Look closely," Ralph instructed. "Even in moments of triumph, the enemy seeks to plant seeds of discord."

The young angels observed as whispers began to circulate among the soldiers. Some praised David's bravery, while others muttered about luck and divine favoritism.

"But David defeated Goliath with faith," Shiloh protested. "Surely that should unite them all?"

Ralph smiled sadly. "Faith can move mountains, yes. But remember, my dear students, humans have free will. They can choose to embrace faith or reject it, even in the face of miracles."

As they watched, David began to walk among the soldiers, offering words of encouragement and praise to God. His humility shone like a beacon, contrasting sharply with the growing undercurrent of jealousy and suspicion.

"This moment," Seymour explained, "is just the beginning. The battle against the corrupting influence of fallen angels will continue throughout human history."

Ralph motioned to the sunset. "Let's move on. There's much more to see."

The scene before them blurred and shifted, colors swirling like paint in water. When it settled, they found themselves in a grand palace, opulent tapestries adorning the walls and the scent of incense hanging heavy in the air.

King Saul sat upon his throne, his face etched with lines of worry and paranoia. David, now a young man, stood before him, a harp in his hands.

"Watch closely," Seymour whispered to Shiloh. "See how the seeds of discord have taken root."

As David's fingers plucked the strings, filling the chamber with soothing melodies, Saul's expression darkened. His eyes darted about nervously, and sweat beaded on his brow.

"The spirit that torments Saul," Ralph explained, "is a direct result of his choices. He has allowed fear and jealousy to consume him, opening the door for darker influences."

Suddenly, Saul's hand shot out, grasping a nearby spear. With a roar of rage, he hurled it at David, who barely managed to dodge the projectile.

Shiloh gasped, his celestial form trembling at the sudden violence. "But why? David serves him faithfully!"

"Precisely," Seymour replied grimly. "Saul fears David's growing popularity and God's favor upon him. The lineage we spoke of earlier? It manifests not just in physical giants, but in the corruption of hearts and minds. By using man's emotional weaknesses and the evil entities that constantly look for weakness to take root and control man's mind and will and soul if it takes deep root."

As David fled the chamber, Ralph turned to his students. "This is but one example of how the influence of fallen beings continues to ripple through human history. It is not always as obvious as a nine-foot giant on a battlefield. Often, it's in the subtle twisting of emotions, the nurturing of fear and hatred."

The young angels watched as David disappeared into the night, his future uncertain but his faith unwavering.

Ralph gestured towards the fleeing David, his eyes filled with compassion. "Now, my dear students, we must follow David's journey. His faith will be tested in ways he cannot yet imagine."

The scene shifted once more, swirling like mist before settling into a rugged landscape of caves and rocky outcrops. David, older now and weathered by hardship, crouched at the mouth of a cave. His loyal men huddled nearby, their faces etched with exhaustion and wariness.

"This is the wilderness of En Gedi," Seymour explained quietly. "David has been forced to flee from Saul's jealous rage."

Shiloh leaned forward, captivated by the determination in David's eyes despite his circumstances. "But he was chosen by God. Why must he suffer like this?"

Ralph placed a gentle hand on Shiloh's shoulder. "Sometimes, young one, the path to greatness is paved with trials. Watch closely."

As if on cue, the sound of marching feet echoed through the canyon. King Saul appeared, leading a contingent of soldiers. Their armor glinted in the harsh sunlight as they searched the area, unaware of how close they were to their quarry.

David's men tensed, reaching for their weapons. But David held up a hand, silencing them. He crept further into the shadows of the cave, his movements careful and deliberate.

"What's he doing?" said Hodge

They watched as Saul, needing rest from the heat of the day, entered the very cave where David and his men were hiding. The tension in the air was palpable as David's followers urged him to strike down the king.

But David's face remained calm, his eyes filled with a mixture of sadness and resolve. He crept forward silently, drawing a small knife. For a moment, it seemed he might give in to the temptation to end his persecution once and for all.

Instead, David merely cut off a corner of Saul's robe before retreating back into the shadows.

"Observe," Ralph said softly. "Even in the face of persecution, David refuses to raise his hand against the Lord's anointed. This is true faith in action."

As Saul left the cave, oblivious to how close he had come to death, David emerged. His voice rang out across the canyon, startling the king and his men.

"My lord the king!" David called out, his voice echoing across the rocky terrain. He held aloft the scrap of fabric he had cut from Saul's robe, the royal purple cloth fluttering in the breeze. With a fluid motion, David bowed low to the ground, his forehead nearly touching the dusty earth.

This gesture of deep reverence demonstrated his unwavering respect for the monarch, despite the years of persecution and hardship that had passed between them. Even now, with Saul's life having been at his mercy, David chose to honor the Lord's anointed rather than seek vengeance.

"Now class you have observed many levels of interaction that might seem a bit strange." said Ralph and continued:

"Through his youth, we witnessed a boy who had known divine safeguarding and blessing. While tending his flock, he'd battled fierce beasts - a lion and bear, lethal hunters that could effortlessly destroy any person. Yet these encounters revealed heaven's shield over David, teaching him absolute faith in his heavenly Fathers care."

"We also observed how man can turn on each other through jealousy and lake of faith in the Father. Saul was a great man of God, but he had drifted into the dark realm by seeking advice and future knowledge through the oracle and this tainted his mind and soul he no longer had a pure heart towards the Farther. His insecurity on who he had become and who David was becoming made Saul hate and fear David, so he tried to kill him."

CHAPTER 7

"I think we will have some great discussions back at the classroom about this adventure said Seymore, smiling back at Ralph.

with that our consoles closed down and we all sat in our chairs not moving all the students were chatting excitedly amongst themselves. i overheard Ralph and Seymore chatting. "It was good to see the battle from another perspective when we were there in real time it was very different." said Ralph,

"Yes, that scroll certainly prepared the students it is a great idea think we will use that again, give them an idea of what to expect." said Seymore

Shiloh drifted back into the battle scene and wanted to absorb it all, faith is so powerful he thought and with the father man can conquer all.

Chapter 8

Creation Bursts Forth in Symphonic Glory

Concealed within the throng that had assembled close to the site of the slaughter, Shiloh's divine essence went undetected by the mortals surrounding him. The warriors under King Saul's command, along with attendants and common people who had observed this momentous occurrence, now mustered the courage to emerge from their sheltered refuge on the hillside.

This surpassed any spectacle he'd witnessed since leaving the Heavenly Realm.

Shiloh found himself captivated by the unassuming shepherd. He remembered Ralph's comments regarding the importance of faith and determination, now embodied in the youthful herdsman standing there.

As the villagers surfaced from hiding, their faces a mix of disbelief and hope, Shiloh sensed a strange sensation. It was as if he could detect the shift in their minds, the reignition of faith that had almost been extinguished by fear. This, he realized, was what Ralph had tried to explain about the impact trials could have on human souls.

Shiloh found himself deeply moved by the scene. He had been created to guide and protect, but witnessing this moment of human triumph made him question the extent of his role. How much of this was divine intervention, and how much was human courage? The lines seemed to blur, and Shiloh felt both humbled and inspired.

As the crowd began to celebrate, Shiloh remained silent and thoughtful. He understood now why his training had been important. The complexities of human life and faith were far more intricate than he had imagined. This event, he realized, wasn't just a victory for David or the Israelites – it was a lesson for him as well.

Shiloh recognized this encounter would remain with him as he persisted in his role as a celestial protector. He had plenty to discover about human resilience and the subtle interplay between divine direction and mortal autonomy. Reinvigorated in his mission, Shiloh braced himself for the challenges awaiting him in his position as a guardian. At that moment, Ralph concluded our simulation and directed us back to our instruction hall. We ambled unhurriedly, still pondering all we had witnessed. It was an indeterminate period later, though time flowed differently in our realm than in this one. We lacked day and night, winter, and summer. We simply progressed from one lesson to the next.

The anticipation in the classroom was palpable as we gathered for our next viewing lesson. Though we simply called it the viewing room, to me, this classroom was a portal to adventure – our launch-pad into the human realm. Here we could travel anywhere along the timeline of Earth and witness the remarkable unfolding of humanity's history.

Seymour elbowed me, his eyes lit with excitement.

"I wonder what earthly wonders we'll explore today?"

I nodded at Seymour, hoping we'd be shown less horrid events, just for a change. Of course, there was no such thing as keeping a secret here and Seymour said, "I think you will enjoy today."

Our teacher, Ralph, quieted the students' general chatter as he stepped before us. His aged, bearded face crinkled into a smile.

"Students, today we embark on a journey, which leads up to a monumental event. You have seen the Father enjoy His creation, Eden, together with Adam and Eve, then you learned about their fall and banishment. Today, however, we will go way back in time, before any of this happened, and witness Creation. And over the next few days, you will see the crowning act in the Father's glorious creation – the moment in which He brings forth humanity."

A murmur rippled through the class. We took our seats, leaning into our screens. Their swirling surfaces held endless possibilities. Where across the ages would they transport us today?

"You will behold how the Father creates light, order and life on earth, and then, finally, shapes Adam, the first man, from the dust of the earth," Ralph said. His voice rang with solemnity.

I readied my scribing tools, heart fluttering in my chest. We were to witness the entire process of Creation as well as the birth of humanity itself. This was a profound gift.

As Ralph instructed us, with a wave of his hand, to activate our screens, the mists cleared to reveal a region at the dawn of life. I leaned forward, sensing the beginning of a sacred story.

"The Father commanded creation of light out of the void that was chaos," Ralph said, "just by speaking the words, "Let there be light!"

My eyes widened as I watched the angels move in unison behind the Holy Spirit. Their forms blurred with the streaks of fire and water swirling in their wake. Creation sprang forth at their touch.

"As the Spirit passes over the waters, notice how matter takes shape," Ralph said, pointing to the deep blues and greens emerging below. "Observe the interplay between the tangible and intangible."

The class murmured in awe. I scribbled notes furiously, trying to capture everything I saw.

"In the beginning, the earth was formless and empty. Darkness was over the surface of the deep, and the Spirit of God was hovering over the waters," Ralph recited.

As he spoke each word, our surroundings transformed. The swirling abyss took on dimension and structure. Light pierced through the void, separating day from night. How could such order arise from chaos? The spectacle was awe-inspiring to witness.

Ralph smiled at our rapt faces. "On the first day, the Father spoke light into existence. With each new day, He will speak new life."

I bounced in my seat, unable to contain my excitement. If this was only the first day, I could hardly imagine what else the Father had in store.

"What comes next?" Jasper asked.

Ralph's eyes twinkled. "Ah, you'll have to wait for tomorrow's lesson."

A collective groan arose from the class. We pleaded for more, but Ralph just chuckled.

"Patience, young ones. Creation cannot be rushed. Return tomorrow and you'll see the next phase unfold."

We filed out, buzzing with questions about what mysteries the remaining days might reveal. The world, which would be peopled by humans, was being shaped before our eyes, and I could not wait to witness more.

The following day brought more surprises.

CHAPTER 8

A hush fell over the classroom as we gathered. Today we would witness the next phase of creation unfold before our eyes.

"Students, prepare yourselves for wonders," Ralph said, his voice tinged with excitement. "When we gathered yesterday, the Father had brought forth light. Now He creates the firmament, and so continues the majestic symphony of creation."

I leaned forward, scribing tools in hand, ready to document every detail. Beside me, Seymour vibrated with anticipation.

"How will it look, this firmament, I wonder?" he whispered.

"I can imagine," I replied. "But I bet it shall be glorious."

A hushed anticipation fell over the classroom as the second day of creation began. We crowded around shimmering mists, ready to witness the Father's next glorious act.

At His booming command, an enormous dome took shape within the swirling void. Molten and metallic, it descended with unexpected speed. I gasped as the colossal firmament drove into the fledgling earth with a tremendous roar. For a moment, all was chaos and thunder.

Then, slowly, the tremors subsided. The magnificent dome settled into a ring of white at the edges of the landmass, hissing and steaming. Perspiration beaded my brow just witnessing the forces at play.

"Behold, the firmament!" Ralph proclaimed, his eyes bright with wonder. "Observe how it forms an enclosure to separate the waters above from those below. See how it breathes life into the planet, giving rise to an atmosphere capable of sustaining life?"

The clanging and scraping sounds of the firmament being established resonated through the heavens. I was amazed, seeing fiery vapour spew, as the icy foundations anchored into place. Within this protective atmosphere, the scene was set for all the plants and animals, and mankind's habitation.

I scribbled notes in fervent astonishment. The firmament undulated like a giant lung around the earth. Within its nurturing embrace, an environment suitable to sustain living beings took shape. It was frightening and beautiful all at once. The Father's power was beyond comprehension.

At his decree on Day Three, apocalyptic sounds erupted. Mighty oceans churned as waters were driven back. Peaks ripped through the surface, snow-capped and jagged, while yawning valleys split open between them. Lands previously submerged arose, draining seas in their wake. The planet convulsed in upheaval at the Father's command.

When, finally, the chaos settled, vast continents stood where once there had only been ocean. Mountain ranges stretched to touch the firmament's roof, yet they were like anthills on the vastness of the landmass and beneath the gigantic firmament. The highest mountains were crested in glistening white. Deep seas teemed between the landmasses, their deep, rich blues providing a vision of serenity after the creative tumult.

Then, in an instant, green growth carpeted the barren ground in emerald hues. Sprouts unfurled and trees stretched their limbs heavenward, dripping with fruit. It was a symphony of growth and colour erupting before us.

I noted with awe the care evident in the Father's craftsmanship. Each plant grew according to its own kind – apple seeds yielding apples, acorns generating oaks. A divine order permeated everything.

We streamed eagerly into the classroom on the fourth day, to hear the Father's voice resounding through the portal, infusing the dome with special new forms of light and dark.

"Let there be lights in the sky's expanse to separate the day from the night!"

Gasps arose from the class, as arrays of light suffused the dome with blinding radiance. Balls of burning gas ignited into being, scattering across the arched expanse like flaming jewels. They ranged in size from small flickering embers to massive swirling giants.

"Those are called stars!" Ralph proclaimed.

As we watched, two larger orbs took shape – one to govern the day, and one to rule the night. The brighter orb blazed with brilliant intensity until it became too bright to look upon directly. The softer orb glowed pale and lustrous, illuminating the night sky.

"The greater light we call the sun, and the lesser light, the moon," Ralph declared.

The Father surveyed his handiwork and saw that it was good. The heavens now glittered with lamps to mark the passage of days and seasons.

Ralph turned to us, his eyes dancing. "Tomorrow brings the fifth day, where winged and aquatic life shall abound at the Father's command. Until then, bask in the glory created thus far."

We left the Great Hall in awe, our imaginations ignited with ideas about the splendours to come. The creation story was just beginning, and I could not wait to witness what future lessons held.

My hand flew across my scroll, struggling to keep pace as Creation unfolded before my eye's day by day. With mere words, the Father sculpted reality from a void on a scale beyond comprehension. Entire landscapes sprang to life at his command.

I stole a glance at Seymour beside me. His enchanted scribe tool documented everything without him even needing to hold it while I scribbled furiously.

He gave me a smug grin. "Patience, Shiloh. In time, you'll record events with the ease of the scribes before you. But for now, keep writing!"

I nodded and refocused my efforts, determined not to miss anything. What we had witnessed today was too important to forget. I went through my notes and read them out loud so I would not miss a beat.

The fifth day began.

"God's wonders are not yet complete!" Ralph cried. "For, next come living creatures, to fill the skies and waters." "Which we will witness today."

The angels circled the portal's edge above in great anticipation. What astonishing designs would the Father conceive next? The air hummed with possibility. We did not have to wait.

"On the fifth day", the Father proclaimed, "Let the earth bring forth life!" His voice cascaded like rolling thunder.

"Behold the next wonder – the living creatures of the sea!" Ralph cried.

At the Father's bidding, the waters teemed with schools of fish, pink coral reefs, and rainbow seashells. Playful dolphins leapt and dived while mighty whales breached the surface in shimmering fountains. The angels sang in joyful chorus at this new gift of life.

Over just a few days, Creation appeared and grew before our eyes on such a vast scale, I couldn't really justify it on parchment or scroll. But there it was.

As I rubbed my aching writing hand, I felt humbled to be required to record such wonders. The creation story was only beginning, and each moment challenged my limited understanding. I yearned to grasp all the Father imagined into being.

What glories waited as the story continued? I poised my pen, eager to document whatever lay ahead. With reverence, I gave myself over to bear witness.

The following day was the day that answered the big why? Why build this wonderful world? Well, here goes.

A hushed reverence filled the classroom as we prepared to witness the wonders of the sixth day of creation. Ralph stood before us, hands clasped, his face glowing with excitement.

"Students, the living creatures brought forth today will showcase the majesty of the Father's imagination," he said. "Observe, for you will see beasts great and small!"

Truly, today, the sixth day, turned out to be the most incredible yet. As morning dawned, I saw God begin to form all the wild beasts and livestock, each according to their unique and perfect designs. My angel brothers and I marvelled at the imagination of our Maker, who could dream up the majestic lion and the gentle lamb, the towering giraffe and the scurrying mouse. The earth teemed with life and creation sang praises to its Author.

As the Father's voice thundered in command, the earth sprang to life. Creatures emerged in astounding variety – massive elephants with trunks that swished through the air. I remembered seeing one on that first visit to earth, on Humba's back. Now there were zebras and giraffes with necks that stretched on forever, and fat, lazy hippos that yawned wide to reveal enormous jaws. The winged creatures, who had been created the previous day, were excited to greet the newcomers. Bright tropical ones, such as I had also seen on my first visit, fluttered overhead, flashing brilliant plumes of sapphire, emerald, and ruby.

"Behold the imagination of our Father!" Ralph cried out jubilantly. "See how each creature is perfectly designed – the thick hide of the rhinoceros, the keen sight of the eagle, the speed of the cheetah? All have their purpose!"

The Father had designed everything so that life begat life. But there was a warning too – "Only like kinds reproduce together in harmony" Ralph said, his eyebrows raised. "There was no disorder or corruption mixing the Father's perfect lines – none of what you saw in the lesson (I'm sorry to have to mention it, but you need the comparison) showing you the fallen angel's evil manipulation of the king for his daughter's hand."

Ralph was right. None of us wanted to be reminded of that lesson. What we were seeing was to be a world of splendour, not chaos. The Father's authority rang clear in the emerging landscape, right down to the last detail.

I scribbled furiously to document it all – the playful antics of monkeys swinging through trees, the majestic stride of lions on the prowl, the earth-shaking footsteps of dinosaurs thundering past. The sheer diversity was astounding.

As the skies filled with honks, chirps and roars, Seymour leaned close and said, "Just imagine, soon we meet Creation's finale – mankind!"

I nodded, buzzing with anticipation. How would the pinnacle of God's creation be made?

Ralph allowed us a moment to process the spectacle before pressing pause.

"Students, did you spy me amongst the heavenly host?" he asked, eyes twinkling.

CHAPTER 8

We burst into laughter at the sight of our mentor looking youthful, compared to his usual, aged appearance.

"Sir, you look so handsome without your long beard!" Seymour blurted out.

Ralph chuckled. "We angels can appear in any age we like. Over time, your experiences shape your wisdom – and your appearance."

I nodded, thinking how ancient Ralph seemed now, compared to my fledgling self. I had much learning ahead.

By now I was almost as good as Seymour in guiding my pen to write superior context super-fast. I was so enthralled in watching the scenes emerge and then evolve, one after the other.

I had barely been able to contain my excitement as I'd peered down from heaven at the new world our Creator was forming. When God said, "Let there be light!" on that first day, I'd watched in awe as light burst forth and divided day from night. The following days had been just as wondrous, as God had separated the seas from the sky and filled the earth with plants and animals of every kind.

And now, just when I might have thought God's ingenuity was spent, He declared to all the congregation looking on, all the angels, the elders, the creatures, everybody looking over the platform into the portal and looking down onto the earth, and to all already there, He said, "Let Us make man in Our image and Our likeness."

"Everything We have created here is for this one created miracle, man," He explained. "He will have a limited lifespan here on earth. He will not live forever in the form that We are making now. But he will live forever in the spirit, in the same type of form that you angels are – excepting that he will have an earthly shell, so to speak, like tortoise over there, or the conker shell, or the clam in the seas. I want there to be a season for him in his existence, to be here on this earth, to face up to various trials and tribulations, to make a final decision. Does he want to come home or not?"

The Father, in an instant, was upon the earth's surface. The red soil shimmered as He landed, and walked over to a spot that He had chosen as a designated spot. He reached down into the soil and put His hands into it, and as He lifted both His hands, the soil grains and sand and all the components in the soil filtered through His hands, and as it fell back onto the ground, a cloud of dust rose. A man's face appeared as the dust and sand and particles fell – all fell into place to form his nose, his mouth, his cheekbones, then his ears, then his forehead and his entire head, with the back of his skull and then his neck, as the Father ran His hand across, indicating the size of the man He wanted, roughly 6 feet tall. A man was formed out of the earth. Every part of his body was perfect, but it lay still. The Father looked down at His creation and looked up at all of us and said,

"This is man. I created this place for him. This man will be the start of great things."

And with that, He lifted the man's head, cradled it in His two hands, and blew His breath into the nostrils of the man. Thus, he breathed Life's essence through the man's nostrils, filling his lungs. The man's eyes opened, and he was alive.

The Father and Adam gazed at each other. As they did so, the Father downloaded all the information into Adam that he needed to thrive and stay alive. There was a connection, an internal connection, a connection that man would never forget and would never be able to satisfy any other way, except through knowing the Father.

Love – that was it. It was divine Love.

I looked across at Seymour. His head was bent and I saw a tear trickle down his face. He looked back at me and grinned and tried to hide the tear.

I said, "Seymour, this is amazing. This is what love is. Look at the way they gaze into each other's eyes. There is depth to it, locking in its immense, incredible, real power. I remember tasting that when the Father first created me and held me in His hands, just like He held Adam in the dirt and He spoke all those blissful things into my being – that I would be a mighty Angel, a mighty Guardian Angel."

We looked back to earth, and saw the Father was still staring into Adam's being. There was a connection. We saw blue light and yellow light and white light passing from one to another, and then, man just said, "Father. Abba, Abba Father."

"Yes, Adam," said the Father, "I am your Father. I am your creator. From this day forth you will be known as Adam, and I call you Adam and name your kind man, of which kind you are the firstborn."

The man, called Adam, arose and gazed in wonder at the world around him. He stretched and moved around. He looked down at his body, looked down at his feet, his legs, his arms, and moved them about. Each time he moved about, he had an inherent recognition that it was all working, and he knew why it worked, and what the legs were for and what each part of his body was for, and how it operated. He turned his head and smiled at the Father.

How special Adam was, made in God's image! I was awestruck. God had endowed Adam with instant knowledge about how to care for the animals and plants in the Garden of Eden. Watching Adam take delight in naming each creature made me smile.

CHAPTER 8

But God was not done. Seeing Adam's loneliness, God said, "It is better for Adam to have a companion, to share all this We have created. They can have shared dominion over all of it and enjoy it together."

I watched with bated breath as God caused a deep sleep to fall upon Adam. Then God took one of Adam's ribs and fashioned it into the most stunning creature I had ever seen. As she was brought to Adam, I could feel the delight radiating from them both. Adam gazed at the new person, so like him yet so different. "Bone of my bones and flesh of my flesh!" he exclaimed. "She shall be called Woman, for she was taken out of Man."

Eve, blinking as if waking from the deepest dream, looked around in awe. I felt her joy as she saw the animals, trees, and flowers for the first time. She turned to Adam with a smile that lit up the whole garden. Adam took her hand, the smile on his face matching hers.

These two humans found in each other what all of Creation was yearning for – a perfect companion. Their hearts overflowed. They rejoiced in each other and in the wondrous world God had made for them.

I was filled with inexpressible gladness. The connection between Adam and Eve seemed to complete all of Creation. I sensed a powerful connection between the first man and woman. I realised they would propagate generations of humanity to dwell in the magnificent world God had crafted. Their love would multiply and fill the earth. Gazing at these first humans, I praised God for the masterpiece of His creation.

I paused in my note-taking, reflecting on everything we had witnessed.

"The massive scope of God's efforts to have created a perfect world for humans is astonishing," I thought. "What a pity they fall from this state of grace. We angels have been given the profound responsibility now, having to guide human souls back to heaven after their time on a corrupted earth, so different from this original Creation."

I looked over at Seymour, who also seemed deep in contemplation.

"What are you thinking about?" I asked him.

"I can't stop thinking about all the souls who don't make it back to heaven," he replied worriedly. "How sad God must feel about every soul that doesn't return, despite everything He's done. Are we angels somehow responsible when that happens?"

"I don't think they can blame us if we do our best to protect and guide each soul," I said. "And remember, there's a lot we can do to help them find their way."

Ralph, who'd overheard our conversation, nodded in agreement.

"You must use every resource available amongst us angels – the bowmen, saboteurs, healers, providers – to assist your human charges," he advised us all, "Now that you have seen how precious they are to the Father. You must respect their free will, but always guide them as close to the light as you can."

Turning to Seymour, I remarked on how everything in creation centred around fellowship between God and humanity. The Father's love for people was so evident in the wonders He had formed for their benefit. I told Seymour that despite life's complexities, each soul's salvation boiled down to one simple choice – to accept and love God or reject Him eternally.

Observing Creation taking shape, I had gained renewed awe for the Father's purposes. He desired intimate friendship with the people made in His image. We angels had been given the profound privilege of guiding human souls into eternal life with their Creator.

We left the classroom with our heads spinning from all the majesty of our Fathers creativity, and gathered in small groups, to discuss various scenes that had mesmerised, overwhelmed and awed us all.

Chapter 9

The Call to Adventure

The next day, Seymour appeared at my side with a glint in his eye. He placed a hand on my shoulder and said, "Alright, Shiloh, it's time we got you properly equipped. We need to get you one of these special vests. You and I, we're going to need every advantage we can get, including the ability to vanish from sight at the touch of a button. It's crucial if we're going to succeed in our mission of guiding lost souls back to heaven."

He paused, his expression growing serious. "You know we'll have to face those fallen ones, right? We must protect the souls in our charge at all costs. It won't be easy, but I have faith in you." Then, his face softened into a warm smile. "Yes, my little Shiloh, we'll work together as a team. And you know what? Despite the challenges, I promise you we'll have some fun along the way. This is what we were created for, after all."

"Ok, young un," I teased him, my eyes twinkling with a mix of amusement and curiosity, "as you seem to always know what's needed and how to do these things – explain to me why it will be fine for us to break away from the rest of the group. Go ahead, enlighten me on your grand plan to cross heaven, sneaking past the celestial guards and cherubim, all the way to the barracks to get it – how, I do not even want to know, but yes, get this vest. And don't think I haven't noticed how rare and coveted it is. I know it is not given to every class member, not even to the most distinguished graduates. Even the teacher, bless his angelic heart, does not have one! Go on then, my brilliant young leader, enlighten me as to how you believe we can accomplish such an audacious endeavor without disturbing the celestial order?

"Well," retorted Seymour, "that is certainly a long-winded way of saying you're not ready yet, sir! I think I need more training, sir," he replied with a challenging grin that stretched from ear to ear. His words carried a playful mockery, gently ribbing my ambitious plan.

"Ok, so how then?" I replied, trying to protect my dignity and maintain my composure in the face of his teasing. I crossed my arms, feigning nonchalance, but inside I felt a twinge of embarrassment at having my grand scheme so easily dismantled. Still, I wasn't ready to give up just yet. There had to be a way to make this work, didn't there?

"After class, we'll head over to the celestial library to delve into any historical lesson we choose and study it in depth. We can't physically attend the actual event, of course, since Ralph won't be accompanying us. But we have the freedom to explore and learn whatever we think is necessary for our growth," replied Seymour, my grinning comrade and mentor, his eyes twinkling with excitement.

"That's quite clever, even bordering on wise," I conceded, nodding appreciatively. "But surely we could find a way to go in person, couldn't we? I mean, physically attend the event somehow?"

"Hmm, well, yes, I suppose that might be possible," Seymour smiled, a mischievous glint in his eye, "but trust me on this one, Shiloh. You'll thank me later, because what I have in mind will be more than just a lesson – it'll be a grand adventure. Sometimes, the most profound experiences come from unexpected places." He paused, his expression softening as he placed a hand on my shoulder. "Remember, my young friend, our role as guardian angels isn't just about witnessing history, but understanding its impact on the souls we're meant to guide. The celestial library offers us a unique perspective that even being present at an event might not provide. We'll see the ripples of history, the consequences that unfold over time. That's where the real wisdom lies."

"An adventure," I mused, my eyes widening with curiosity. "I thought that was man's term for a new experience! Are we angels adopting human phrases now?"

"Yeah, we need to experience a fresh perspective, so we can truly understand our charges," Seymour explained, a hint of excitement in his voice. "It's not just about observing from afar; we need to immerse ourselves in their world, feel what they feel."

I furrowed my brow, a mixture of concern and amusement crossing my face. "You have been hanging around man too much," I worried, my voice tinged with a touch of playful accusation. "It is affecting you, Seymour. I can hear it in your words. How many times have you been down there to help look after a man's soul? It seems like you've picked up quite a few of their mannerisms."

Seymour shifted uncomfortably, "Hmm, I have not got permission to discuss such things with an underling," he replied, his tone suddenly formal and awkward. The abrupt change in his demeanor only piqued my curiosity further, making me wonder just how much experience he truly had with the mortal realm.

"You are just too much sometimes," I protested. "First, you want to be my partner, and then you want to be my senior and have me go off the grid to have a little fun."

"Oh, excuse me, young un," Seymour remonstrated in turn, "but you need me. I am your best chance of having a successful return."

At that, I turned and left Seymour standing alone at the edge of the portal.

The thought of having that vest – whatever it was – seemed to be an added insurance for my success. Yes, I wanted it, and I was sure it would help. But it was the sneaky tactics that bothered me. Sure, we were to be bold and even brave and beat the enemy at his own game, but I did not want to change my heart or my dignity.

"Shiloh, can I have a word with you please?" asked Ralph, who suddenly appeared, out of nowhere.

"Hmm?" I asked, a little dazed.

"Young Shiloh I have a few questions to ask you about our last trip. Do you mind if I walk with you?" asked Ralph.

"Ok, sir, but I am not sure of anything anymore. There seem to be more variables than I thought."

"Yes, Shiloh, it is hard to understand it all, but you will get there. Remember, Seymour has done protection duty many times, and he has done it for real on four trips. Three were with me. I was his senior, and I was hard on him, hehe, I did not let him get away with anything. Especially when it came to collecting all the extra equipment needed to secure victory. Yes, Shiloh, we are bound by rules and regulations, and we may not get caught breaking them."

Ralph looked at me with upturned eyes as he bowed his enormous head.

"So, getting to your opinion of the lesson on the temptation and the fall of man. What did you think of the adversary, Lucifer?"

"Well, sir, he seemed to be manipulative and crafty, if those are the correct words. He twisted everything, and he seemed to use emotions and other feelings that Adam had, to get him to break his word with the Father. I guess it was that pride that everyone talks about," I continued, with Ralph listening closely. "The cause of the war seems to be everywhere down there. Especially when the grace was lifted. Everything became so different. One second there was calm and peace, in the next, violence and death, and other deep, dark forces surfacing. The control over the animals, even – I did not know that the authority that Adam had was over the realm to the fullest degree."

"Yet when he disobeyed out of pride and greed, he lost everything. I also could feel the shame he felt when he saw the Father in the clearing. The Father's pain and disappointment were so hard to ignore," I went on, encouraged by Ralph's interest in my observations. "He was the creator of everything, and He seemed to be overcome with grief and pain. Sorrow and, wow, it is so hard to understand – the Father is so above everything, even emotions, yet He loved Adam so much that He needed to reflect that pain and sorrow and grief, so Adam could digest the truth."

Ralph waited for more, he seemed to take stock of my answer.

"Sir, I will get the extra equipment, so I can defend my charge better," I proclaimed, "and I am committed to the rules."

"Good, Shiloh, you have my blessing. Take this card with you, it will get you in and out. I bet Seymour does not have one." Ralph grinned and vanished.

Well, that was a real unravelling of the rule book for me. We were supposed to be angels bound to the rules of the order we belonged to, which for me was the guardian's order. Yet, our priority was to succeed, regardless of any order. It felt like stepping into uncharted territory, a realm where the black and white of angelic law blurred into shades of gray. I couldn't help but wonder if this flexibility was a test of our judgment or a necessary innovation of the rules, in the complex tapestry of human existence. The weight of this revelation settled on my shoulders, a mix of exhilaration and trepidation coursing through my celestial being.

I had learned so much thus far, through the many strange feelings I had been exposed to. I felt both daunted and excited by my future responsibilities.

Seymour materialized next to me with a small, weathered bag of goodies slung casually over his shoulder, his eyes twinkling with anticipation. The sudden appearance of my mentor startled me for a moment, but his warm presence quickly put me at ease. "So, young Shiloh," he said, his voice filled with a mixture of excitement and gentle encouragement, "are you ready to embark on that adventure with me?" My guardian's invitation hung in the air, tantalizing and full of promise. I could sense that this journey would

CHAPTER 9

be unlike anything I had experienced in my training thus far, and a thrill of anticipation coursed through me.

"Indeed, ancient one," I retorted, "though perhaps not quite as sagacious as you'd like. What's that delightful aroma, Seymour? What treasures are you concealing in that satchel?" I inquired of my now quieted companion.

"Well, we need to offer a gift to get past the gate, and that is one sure gift that will get us in."

"What is it?"

"They call this sweetie or, you might have heard the term, honey."

"Honey, I thought that was a man thing. Why bring it into our realm?"

"Oh, young un," Seymour was in his authority again, "you have a lot to understand. The man's realm is a shadow of our realm. We have all, and I mean: all the good stuff here in our realm. And there is no deterioration or fault to it. So, the honey here is perfect, and it never goes grainy or crystalline, it always gives you a rush, yeah, rush. That is why it is so prized in the army sector. It gives them a boost. We do need to be careful that only the right angel gets it. If we get one like me, well, I think that could get messy," he joked, chuckling to himself. "Here, try some."

He opened the sackcloth, and there it was – a sticky, sweet-smelling goo.

I took my finger and dipped it into the honey. It was soft and sticky, and I took a deep whiff. Wow, it sang a song or rhyme, which seemed short and full of vibrant colours. I put it into my mouth, and its taste exploded as if my whole body vibrated.

"Whooh, that was different. Are you going to have some?" I asked Seymour, still feeling the vibrant sensations of the honey coursing through my body. My tongue tingled with the lingering sweetness, and I couldn't help but wonder how it would affect an angel like him.

"Me, oh no, I get way too adventurous! Hehehe," he laughed, his eyes twinkling with mischief. "Last time I tried it, I ended up doing loop-de-loops through the clouds for hours. It's best I stay grounded... well, as grounded as an angel can be!"

We'd made our way back to the portal while talking, our footsteps light and quick with excitement. Just as we stepped to its edge, our light boards appeared in a shimmer of golden radiance, hovering expectantly before us. Without hesitation, we hopped on, the familiar warmth of divine energy pulsing beneath our feet. With a shared grin of anticipation, we leaned forward and off we flew, soaring through the ethereal landscape towards the far end of the realm. The wind of heaven rushed past us, carrying whispers of celestial melodies as we zipped across the expanse of light and wonder.

That was truly an extraordinary day for me, one I'll never forget. It marked the first time I had laid eyes on such a vast expanse of what would become humanity's future dwelling place. As we soared through the air, we passed by an impressive mountain range, its slopes steep and adorned with an array of vibrant, swaying ferns. These mesmerizing plants seemed to beckon us closer, their gentle movements inviting us to join them in their celestial dance.

"What is that?" I asked in awe, my gaze fixed on a seemingly endless slope that stretched out before us. It was a breathtaking sight, towering at least 500 feet high and disappearing into the distance. As we drew nearer, the soft whisper of the breeze passing through the ferns reached our ears, creating a sweet, enchanting melody that filled the air around us. The ferns continued their rhythmic waving, urging us onward as if eager to share their secrets. With graceful precision, our light boards glided effortlessly over the topmost ridge of ferns, allowing us to experience their beauty up close as we continued our heavenly journey.

Then Seymour said, "Let's do it, young un, let's ride the wave. It's time to show you one of the most exhilarating experiences an angel can have."

"Wave, what wave?" I asked, my brow furrowing in confusion as I scanned the endless sea of ferns before us.

But Seymour was already in motion, his form fluid and graceful as he hugged the side of the cliff-face. He picked up speed with astonishing swiftness, his light board gliding effortlessly over the terrain. Stretching his arm out, he let his hand glide over the tips of the fronds, creating a ripple effect in his wake. To my amazement, the plants seemed to come alive, their delicate leaves quivering with what could only be described as pure joy. They were shrieking with delight as he sped past, their voices a melodious chorus that filled the air.

Down he moved, his body in perfect harmony with the undulating landscape, then up again in a graceful arc. Suddenly, he rose abruptly further up, his movements precise and controlled. In a breathtaking maneuver, he turned upside down, his light board suspended in the air above him like a halo. With expert timing, he reached out and grabbed a frond, using it to pivot and propel himself back down again. The entire display was a mesmerizing dance between angel and nature, leaving me in awe of Seymour's skill and the wondrous world around us.

CHAPTER 9

"Come on, Shiloh, try it, this is great."

I looked down the steep slope and noticed a tiny house at the bottom, with a neat fence-line and trees. But it was so far down, and it seemed delicate and tiny. As I travelled along the cliff, I realized why it looked so small. Yes, it was tiny because the cliff-face was so steep and high and long. I could make out Seymour as he grew smaller and smaller, but he was enjoying a splendid ride. My board glided over the fronds. The ferns spoke out. "Yeah, come on, young un, you will love it, we enjoy it when you ride our wave, just go as fast as you want and use your legs to control those radical turns."

I smiled at the ferns and said I would enjoy this, and, holding my breath, I flew over.

The board screamed in delight, and I leaned into the side. As I looked up, I could see the ferns waving at me, encouraging me to go even faster. Along the cliff-face I moved, and as I pushed down on my right leg, the board rose up – wow, then I put pressure on the left leg and we went down. Up and down, till I was really in a rhythm, and then I pressed hard on my back right foot and I shot up to the top and passed over a wall. I continued up and over. Then I descended and when I reached the bottom, I shot past the house that was not so tiny anymore, along the road, to the top of the fence and then, faster, back up again. Seymour was waiting on top of the cliff-face.

"See, I told you, isn't it amazing? And look how you mastered your wave-jumping on your first try. You sure learn fast," Seymour said.

"Yes," I said, breathless from the exhilaration, "It was the best, I loved the feeling when I glided down the cliff-face and leaned into the ferns, yeah, even what they say and sing is classic. One even said yeah," I laughed, my whole body still tingling from the rush. "The way the wind rushed past my face, and how everything blurred into a kaleidoscope of colors – it was incredible. I never imagined I could feel so free, so alive. And those ferns, they're not just plants, are they? It's like they have their own personalities."

"Well, we are about halfway now. Do you want to get there soon, or shall we explore some more?" asked my guardian, his voice carrying a hint of amusement at my obvious excitement.

"Hey," I replied with fresh zeal, without knowing or even caring where we were 'halfway' to, "let's explore some more, we don't need to rush this outing. There's so much to see and experience!"

Down the back end of the cliff-face we continued, The air grew cooler and more humid as we dropped in altitude. Eventually, we came to a large lake, whose pristine blue water was like a flawless mirror, greeting us with a breathtaking reflection of the sky above. The surface was so still it seemed almost solid, broken only by the occasional ripple from a gentle breeze.

There was a group of big-built angels gathered at the water's edge, their imposing figures standing out against the serene backdrop. They had shiny belts that held long scabbards with intricate engravings and writing on them, each one unique and telling its own story. The light glistened off the hilts, creating a dazzling display of celestial craftsmanship. These angels exuded an air of authority and purpose, their very presence commanding respect and awe.

"Hey, you two, come down," called out one of the largest angels I have ever seen. His arm muscles rippled and had gold and silver bands with writing on them, covering his upper arm, and he wore wider and heavier-looking bands over his strong forearms. His hand was on the hilt of his sword that was still held in its scabbard.

"Come on, we don't like onlookers we don't know."

With that, we glided down to the party of warriors. We hopped off our boards and addressed the group.

"We are from the guardians," started Seymour.

"Ha ha ha," went up a communal chuckle.

"Yes, we can see that," said the leader, leaning down to inspect my perplexed face.

"What are you two doing so far from the comforts of home?" asked the leader.

"Hmm, well, you see, we were considering it a great idea if we could trade some of this for a vest," said Seymour, shuffling his feet in the soft sand.

There was complete silence. The angels just stood there, staring at us.

Seymour glanced at me with a concerned frown, and then the leader said,

"You want a vest, hey, and you think a little sweetie will get you one. I see you already have one Mr Seymour. I take it this is your apprentice," he added, as he motioned towards me with a large, ringed finger.

"Yes, sir, this is Shiloh, and we will, as you know, have to go on a mission when we finish school. You know how important the vest is," Seymour declared bravely.

"Yes, we do, master Seymour, but sweetie will only buy you the way in, not the vest," said the leader, adding, "Today, you will need to earn the vest."

"That's not our usual arrangement," protested Seymour.

"If you can't prove you need the vest and that you will not abuse the privilege of wearing it, then you can't have it. Those are new regulations," the leader of the warrior angels, who were all bowmen, said.

CHAPTER 9

"Ok, what do we have to do?" Seymour asked.

"We were just discussing how we could practice chasing each other, and Herman here needs to perfect the art of shooting arrows with that bow."

The leader gestured toward an enormous golden bow that seemed to shimmer and undulate before a towering, muscular angel. I found myself marveling at how challenging it must be to move swiftly with such an impressive physique when suddenly, I realized with a jolt that every single one of them could hear my inner musings as clearly as if I had spoken aloud. The revelation sent a wave of embarrassment washing over me.

"Hehe," chuckled the leader, his eyes twinkling with amusement. "You need to master the art of controlling your thought patterns and learn to think with clarity, young one. We've been privy to the meanderings of your little mind for quite some time now, which puts you at quite the disadvantage in our company." He grinned broadly, nodding his head knowingly as if sharing a secret joke. "Allow me to introduce myself properly. I'm the leader and instructor of this fine group, and you may address me as Mac."

Feeling a mix of curiosity and slight unease, I gathered my courage and posed the question that had been nagging at me since our arrival. "If you don't mind me asking, Mac, how exactly do you know my friend, Seymour?" I inquired, my gaze darting between the imposing leader and my familiar companion.

"Well, Seymour was in the first class that Ralph took. I believe it was class 15, and Ralph, well, he could have been a class of his own. We have some great stories about him. One day, he brought Seymour to us and asked if he could be given some extra training. Hehe," Mac chuckled, before continuing. "Seymour is quite exceptional. He has an adventurous streak in him that always seems to get him into, well, say a tight spot from time to time. He loves antagonising the enemy, and he is superb at reading the enemy and setting traps for him. When you are in the field, it is not like it is here. There is much happening, and the enemy is busy, always trying to bring your man's soul down. Breaking the man is their game. But we are there too, and we dislike the enemy. So, we have what are known as confrontations.

"We can't kill each other," he went on, "it's not like when man fights. That is scary. They get hurt and bleed and die. Our attacks are at another level. But we do our best to deflect the enemy, and your job, young one, is to protect your charge, and that is where your training is needed. The school can only teach you so much, but you can, if you want to, learn a lot more. Do you have the card?" he asked me, stretching out his arm.

I put it into his hand, and he looked at it, and then at me, and after a while he nodded.

Seymour had been eyeing us out from across a big, fallen tree. Now he came to stand alongside Mac.

"So, you did not tell me you got a card, hey," he grinned with a nod of approval. "I guess Ralph sees you have potential," he said. Looking at Mac, he asked, "What does it say?"

"Never you mind, master Seymour. But the two of you make a great team," Mac acknowledged his approval.

We all gathered around the tree trunk. It lay half on the shore and half in the lake. Mac ordered everyone to pay attention.

"First things first, we need targets, and yes, you guessed it, you two will do nicely. I want you to go out to the end of the trunk, you will take the shields, and I want you to stand four bodies apart. Ok, go now."

We walked to the end of the tree trunk, and Seymour instructed me to be behind him.

"Remember, those arrows are serious, they pack a punch. You need to dodge them, not catch them."

"Right, I guess you have done this before, hey."

"Um, no, not like this, but in the field, I have seen what they can do, and believe me, you do not want to get in their way."

"Great, great idea of yours, this adventure thing, remind me why I came along."

Thwack! came the first one. It landed in the middle of Seymour's shield. He lifted off the trunk and landed on his behind.

"Ouch, man, that was fierce."

The next one flew past and into the water, then the next came straight for me. I threw myself onto the trunk and hugged it. Swoosh, over my back it passed.

"That was close," I said.

Seymour was now concentrating, and he seemed to be able to judge the flight path and was able to deflect them, rather than let them find their mark in his shield.

"Now, Shiloh, your turn, you stand in the front. I want you to consider the arrow as it leaves the bow," he instructed me. "You need to predict its path of flight and your shield needs to be told where to go. Ready, here it comes, right, right."

Thwack! it hit the right corner of my shield and spun me into the air, and off into the lake I went. It was cold, and yes, wet. I know this is obvious, right? But I had never swum before. I thrashed around, my arms instinctively pushed down, and the water seemed to

CHAPTER 9

some extent to hold me up. And then I kicked my legs, and I floated and edged to the tree trunk.

"Project your thoughts, young un, we don't need to learn to swim, just get here, the next salvo will start," warned Seymour.

I did what he demanded and pictured myself on the trunk, dry, I did not enjoy the wet feel. In the next instant, I was standing beside Seymour, dry and smiling.

"Can you swim?" I asked.

"What? No, of course not, why would I want to? Young un, you have a lot to learn, look, just follow my lead."

This time four bowmen fired a salvo towards us. The arrows seemed to sing as they came in fast. I moved next to Seymour, and we instinctively placed our shields together, and I screamed at the shields to fix themselves into the trunk. A wall formed, and we hid behind it. In unison, thump, all four arrows hit the shields, and it did not affect us, as the shields had penetrated the trunk and fixed themselves firmly as a wall.

Seymour grinned, and then the next lot came. We hid behind our wall, and salvo after salvo came in to land. I glanced at the front of the shields, they looked rather strange with all the arrows sticking out.

"Ok, you two, you can come back now," called Mac.

The shields were stuck fast, so I shouted with authority, "Release, I say release! And now return from where you came, now go!"

I commanded them with a deep and strong voice and the shields shot up into the air, and all the arrows shot off back towards the bowmen. They landed in a neat row at the feet of the bowman with a resounding ship-ship-ship.

"That's neat, Shiloh, well done. You two, now come here, and we will discuss the next excursion," said Mac.

Chapter 10

Tests of Mettle

Mac gave me the precious vest, but said it is only on loan for now. I would have to give it back if I did not pass the next test. He instructed us to leave and traverse an open meadow beyond the lake. His bowmen would come looking for us, and if they found us before we surprised him with a covert return, we would fail the test – meaning, I would lose my vest!

The tall meadow grasses swayed around us, brushing against our legs as we ran. Scattered trees and low-lying bushes dotted the landscape. Seymour led the way, his shoulders back and head held high. I followed behind, staring in wonder at the beauty surrounding us. Our light boards floated at our sides, cloaked by invisibility.

Up ahead, the meadow gave way to a small stand of trees and underbrush. The foliage grew denser, offering potential shelter from prying eyes. "We must find a place to hide before Mac's bowmen find us," Seymour declared, his voice low and urgent.

He scanned the area his keen eyes darting from tree to bush, searching for any sign of concealment. Suddenly, he spotted a ditch, half-concealed by hanging vines and overgrown vegetation. Crouching down, he approached and pulled back the curtain of leaves, revealing a dark, mysterious tunnel leading deep underground. The entrance visible, hidden by nature's own camouflage.

We glanced at each other, The tunnel's mouth gaped before us like a black void, promising secrets, and potential dangers. Neither of us relished the idea of descending into the unknown depths, where who knows what creatures or obstacles might await.

CHAPTER 10

The damp, earthy smell wafting from the opening did little to ease our concerns. But with the bowmen fast approaching, their footsteps echoing in our minds, we knew we had no choice. Time running out, and this hidden passage might be our only chance at evading capture and completing our mission.

Taking a deep breath, I lowered myself into the tunnel, Seymour followed close behind. The earthy passage gave way to an expansive, dark cavern. Dripping water echoed through the chamber and a damp chill permeated the air. I shuddered, my nerves on edge. In the distance, the sound of rushing water beckoned us forward. We hurried across another fallen tree, which served as a makeshift bridge over a flowing, underground river. Its crystal blue waters sparkled alluringly, in the dim light.

I paused to take in the breathtaking sight when a high-pitched shriek pierced the air, causing me to flinch. A flutter of leathery wings swooped past us as one bat, then another, took to the air in a flurry of movement. Within moments, they filled the cavern with their shrill cries, using echolocation to navigate the inky darkness that surrounded us.

"They're mapping the cave with sound!" Seymour said, "The bowmen will have a challenging time tracking us with all this noise and these confusing smells. It's like nature's own security system!"

He cocked his head, listening, his eyes closed in concentration, a grin spread across his face, transforming his serious expression. "They've stopped at the entrance," he whispered. "I think the bats have deterred them! Who would have thought these little flying mammals would be our unexpected allies?"

Relief washed over me like a cool wave, my tense muscles finally relaxing as the immediate danger passed. After confirming the bowmen had retreated, Seymour and I exchanged cautious glances, daring to believe our luck. The echoing squeaks of the bats returned to their normal rhythm, a reassuring soundtrack to our narrow escape. I took a deep breath, inhaling the damp, musty air of the cave, grateful for its sanctuary. we left the cave's shelter. I emerged, caked in grime, trying to brush off the pungent bat guano coating my hands. Seymour smiled.

"Breathe deeply and visualise yourself being washed clean," he instructed.

I closed my eyes, taking a calm breath and picturing a wave of light cleansing every inch of my body. A vibrant beam pulsed over me, whisking away all traces of filth.

"Wow!" I exclaimed, examining my now spotless self in amazement.

Seymour nodded but said nothing, allowing me to revel in this latest discovery.

"Wow," I said again, and then asked, though I already knew the answer, "Why did I have to take a deep breath, Seymour?"

He smiled and said, "You still need to hide those little thoughts of yours, Shiloh."

With that, we felt it safe to return to our newfound teacher, Mac.

"That's neat!" I said, still impressed with the new ability I had mastered.

"Mmm," said Seymour, smiling.

Together, we descended the hillside, ready to reunite with Mac and continue our journey.

We descended; however, we realised that still needed to be aware of the bowmen, the chase not over yet. The cave had offered us a convenient distraction, but the bowmen could still track us down.

Seymour motioned to a clearing, where Mac sat waiting on a fallen tree log. He looked bored and whittling a piece of wood with his slim light beam. I leaned closer to Seymour and asked, "What's he doing and what is that he has? I want one."

Seymour chuckled, forgetting our predicament.

"Now, Shiloh, you can't have everything, or you will need a troop of helpers to carry your kit. That, my young friend, is a light beam. It cuts through anything from wood to rock, I've used it to cut out a hole in a mountainside to make a hideout. Well, more of that later we need to get to Mac before the bowmen do," he blurted. "Remember our task!"

We moved towards Mac and Seymour showed me how to engage my vest, so I would not be visible. He raised his fist, and we stopped. He crouched down and pointed. In the distance, we saw the group of bowmen heading towards Mac. We were coming to Mac from the south, while they were moving in from the west. Seymour motioned us forward, and we covered the ground.

Mac looked up and smiled. "Well, you have won."

I looked in confusion at Seymour, who pressed the clip on his vest and appeared next to Mac.

"How did you know we were here?" I asked.

Mac smiled as I pressed my button.

"You see, Shiloh, I have learned many ways to observe my targets. If you rely on one or two senses, then you will limit your abilities. I have placed replicas of my spirit on watch, and I can control their movements with my thoughts. This is an advanced technique, which you are not ready for yet, but I know you will soon be back to learn. You both did well to avoid my bowmen, they are excellent at tracking. Our heroes come!" Mac went

CHAPTER 10

on. "They don't look too pleased with themselves, and I guess it's time for you, Shiloh, and Seymour to go. Well, my heroes, how come you did not find these young angels?" he grinned as his guard of bowmen joined us.

The group shuffled defeat and mumbled under their breath. "Well, Sir, they disappeared down a hole, and we would not find them."

With that, Seymour clipped on the buckle and vanished before their eyes.

"Our friends have extra help," objected Herman, the largest of the bowmen.

"Yes, but they earned it," retorted Mac. "I think it's time for another exercise," he continued. "This time I want you, my mighty heroes, to hide from these two little angels. How does that sound to you guys?" he said, turning to us. "Do you think you will find them, as big as they are? I'm sure you will seek them out."

The bowmen set off across open land and down into the deep valleys into a forest.

"Shiloh, you will lead!" said Mac. "I want to see how well you do. Seymour, you will listen to what Shiloh says – even if he is making a mistake. He needs to learn from experience."

"Yes, sir," said Seymour.

"Can we take the vests?" I asked.

"Yes, you can, Shiloh. Do me a favour," Mac reiterated, "find my bowmen."

Off we went, in the direction we had seen them leave, and I made sure I followed the tracks in the sand and on the ground. The grass, being soft, revealed their path. Every now and again, I stopped and listened, not only with my outer ears, but with my inner ears. I listened to their thoughts, and I heard them every now and again. They came in waves, and I noticed that colours accompanied them. The colours washed over the ground, and the plants absorbed them. So, I worked out that the colours, and the waves, did not last long in the air. That is how I learned to judge the distance they were from us.

As a check, I would look over at Seymour. He knew a lot more than me, and he is bursting to tell me where he thought they were. But this is my leading time, and he honoured that. But he had a tell, and that is how he looked to the left when he noticed something.

I looked at the terrain, I noticed there were streaks of blue and green, like waves that hung above the ground, and they moved in a certain direction, the direction of Mac's bowmen.

There were six distinct rivers of vibrant color that meandered along the ground, their hues shifting and blending as they flowed. Every so often, they would pause and, form a dazzling rainbow of colors that seemed to dance before my eyes. These were the places where the bowmen had stopped to converse, leaving behind an ethereal imprint in the earth. I continued to observe, I noticed the vibrant streams of color diminishing in intensity. The once-brilliant hues slowly lost their luster, becoming muted and subdued. , these ethereal trails began to blend seamlessly with the surrounding terrain, their distinctiveness fading away like a beautiful mirage.

Despite their ephemeral nature, I realized we could still use these fading color paths to our advantage. If we maintained a swift pace, we could follow the remnants of these magical trails before they disappeared. For a brief window of time, these ghostly ribbons of color proved more valuable than traditional footprints in the yielding sand. They offered us a clear and unmistakable path to follow, guiding us through the landscape with an almost supernatural precision.

Seymour's keen eyes caught the same mystical lines, and he turned to me with a wide grin, offering an approving nod as we pursued the bowmen. We crouched in the lush grass, our senses heightened as we watched and waited, feeling their presence in the distance. I made out the origins of their colorful rivers, which appeared to spring forth from the northern slope. I observed more closely, I noticed that these streams split into two separate paths.

"Seymour," I whispered, "I think we need to split up." I paused, formulating a plan in my mind. "If you head east, I'll take the western route. We can then circle around and catch them off guard."

Seymour nodded; his eyes gleaming with understanding. "Alright," he replied, "I'll go east and wait for your signal. You remember how to signal, don't you? Just call my name in your mind alone, and I'll hear you. Then I'll move in and we'll grab them."

With a silent nod of agreement, Seymour slipped away to the east, his form melting into the shadows like mist, while I made my way westward, each step calculated and soundless. We circled for about half a mile, our movements swift and purposeful, our angelic training allowing us to cover ground with supernatural speed and grace. The terrain, challenging, but we navigated it, our senses attuned to every rustle and whisper of the forest.

Soon, we found ourselves positioned above the bowmen, perched on a small ridge that offered an excellent vantage point. they huddled together in two distinct groups, their voices carrying on the night air. Their overconfidence palpable, evident in their relaxed postures and casual conversation. I knew it would be their undoing, a fatal flaw that we can exploit to our advantage. I observed them, I couldn't help but feel a mixture of pity and determination. These men had no idea we were so close and had them in a snare.

We each donned our vests, the material shimmering in the dim light. Moving with practiced stealth, we converged on their position, settling ourselves about thirty yards away from the unsuspecting group. From our vantage point, we can eavesdrop on their conversation, their words drifting to us on the gentle breeze.

Herman, the leader of the archers, explained to the others how clever he is at evading the enemy and how he always knew where the enemy was. He folded back his cloak to reveal silver chainmail that shone in the light. It shone, and the reflections bounced off the side walls of the cliff-face.

Jack, who is to be the rawest recruit, exclaimed, "You will give us away by doing that, look at the walls!"

"Those two Guardian Angels will never find us!" laughed Herman and tossed his head back, shouting out, "Come and get us if you can!"

Up stood Seymour, who I could see now felt determined to prove his worth as a guardian. He walked over and stood above them, flicked the buckle of the vest, and appeared to them.

"Well, now look at you all huddled up together," he said.

"Yes, master Seymour, once again you have surprised me!" said Herman.

I walked over to my group and did the same thing, they were not expecting me, and they took a little while to realise I was standing there.

Clayton, one of Herman's most seasoned archers, raised an eyebrow and questioned me about my sudden materialization. His keen eyes narrowed as he studied me, aware of the cloak's concealing power and its role in their capture. Despite his current predicament, a hint of overconfidence still lingered in his demeanor, a trait that had contributed to their downfall.

He shifted his weight; I couldn't help but notice Clayton's imposing physique. His broad, back rippled with muscle beneath the chameleon-like cloak that draped over his shoulders. The fabric shimmered, adapting to the surroundings in a mesmerizing display of camouflage technology. When he moved again, I caught a glimpse of the intricate chain link armor that hugged his muscular frame, the metallic links glinting in the light. This sight only served to confirm what I already knew - Clayton is a warrior angel, built for combat and trained to perfection. His presence alone spoke volumes about the caliber of Herman's team and the challenges that lay ahead.

"Yes, we've surprised you," I replied, "We have found and captured you, so let's take you back to Mac, without an outright confrontation as you will be the victor, but this is a discover and reveal exercise, not a real one either. Seymour and I bowed our respect evident. and now I will qualify."

"I am sure you will never qualify to be a warrior angel, but you have impressed me and my men," said Herman. "You have earned your vest! However, that is not for me to say," he qualified his praise.

We walked down together to where Mac sat waiting, this time using the open clearing over which the trees towered. It formed a circle of green grass with bluebells and daffodils together, which was dancing to hidden music.

The band of warriors arrived together as a cohesive unit, impressing Mac. He had often emphasized to his men that unity is a powerful force, and here is a prime example of that principle in action. We settled ourselves on the two weathered logs facing Mac, the rough bark pressing against our legs as we awaited his assessment.

"Well, Shiloh and Seymour," Mac began, his piercing gaze moving between us, "you've defied my expectations. Not only have you caught my lead squad, but you've brought them back intact. I'm curious – what gave them away?"

I leaned forward, eager to share our discovery. "It was the rivers of color that their tracks left behind," I explained, my voice tinged with excitement. "The vibrant trails were visible across the ground, revealing not just their movements but also their strategy. I could even pinpoint where they gathered to discuss their next moves and the exact locations where they split up."

Mac nodded before turning his attention to his men. "Now, warriors," he said, his voice carrying a note of challenge, "you've heard what betrayed your position. How do you propose to prevent this from exposing you to the enemy in the future?"

A palpable silence fell over the group as the men exchanged uncertain glances. Clayton's broad shoulders rose in a shrug, while Herman's eyes darted towards me, seeking a solution. The confusion on their faces been evident, highlighting the unexpected nature of this new obstacle.

Seymour, ever the quick thinker, broke the silence with a suggestion. "What if you utilized birds to disrupt the color trails?" he proposed, his voice steady and confident. "You could enlist their help to fly over the paths, scattering and dispersing the colors. This natural camouflage could mask your movements."

CHAPTER 10

"Yes, I suppose that could work, and in an emergency, it is a method we need to remember. This is a good moment to introduce you to another group of warrior angels. We call them saboteurs, or diversionists. But first," he smiled, "I want to congratulate you, Shiloh. You have earned your invisibility vest."

Chapter 11

Dancing for Joy

I was still all warm and glowing with joy, and thanking Seymour, and the bowmen and, of course, my Father, for having helped me to pass all the necessary tests, when two angels appeared next to us.

They wore long, flowing white gowns, and both carried swords, not at their sides, but slung across their backs. The swords were held in place with a wide, embossed band that looked like it had been made from leather, slick, well-oiled, with silver studs forming various patterns, which, at the command of the saboteur, as one of them demonstrated, changed in shape and size.

The saboteurs were large, and they are strong and agile. They showed us how they could call upon their cloaks to stretch out behind them as they moved, and how they absorbed any motion left behind them. The cloaks worked with a sponge effect, dissolving everything. Even the plants that had been bent over by pressure were corrected, and they left no sign at all that there had been a pursuit.

The leader of the saboteurs was named Mark. He had long, flowing hair which was braided on the left-hand side. He had deep blue eyes and what looked like a beard. His chin was covered with silver-white, wispy hair. His beard seemed to move and disappear, grow, and shrink.

The saboteurs differed vastly from the bowman warrior angels and us. They could change their shape, size, colour, or any aspect they wanted to, of the so-called physical body. They could make themselves larger or smaller. By doing this, they could disappear, or, alternatively, appear to be very impressive.

Mark spoke, "The saboteurs' job is to cover your tracks to protect you from behind, but also to go ahead. We can do many things to confuse the enemy's traps and diversions and we confuse him. This gives you opportunities to outwit him. As we follow behind you, we shed our coats, and they float above the ground, and we destroy any evidence of you passing by. The cloaks absorb the colour trail that you leave, so the enemy will never know where you are or where you have been, unless they see you."

"So, how do we call upon you when we are in the field?" asked Seymour.

"We show up in your spirit as you call to the Father. We respond to the Father's orders. Whenever you are in trouble, you can ask for us, and we will be there on His command. Once you have determined where you want to go, we go ahead of you, so that we are there to see if the enemy is there and what traps he has set for you. Understand, he is vigilant and nasty and violent, but he is also careless."

Mark paused, letting his words sink in. Then he continued. "The enemy often places what we call word bombs in the path of man. These are immensely powerful in their effects, and if man is unaware, they will influence him. These words contain fear, intimidation, depression, hopelessness, and so on."

Shiloh asked, "Sir, what would be a common fear word bomb?"

"Well Shiloh, the enemy will seek to exploit man's emotional state and the prior knowledge he has gained to set off the bomb. This could happen when man is confronted with a major decision, both physically and mentally, about whether to go in one direction or another. For instance, he might decide to walk near a cliff edge to bypass an obstacle, when he encounters a word bomb that fills him with fear of falling off the cliff. He can become paralyzed by fear and can then endanger himself and others.

"A more mental example would be when a man needs to make a life-altering decision. Let's say he is considering following the Father and the Fathers ways, and the fear-bomb is activated. He will then experience a rush of thoughts that his life will soon end, that he won't be able to enjoy his life, that he will suffer and be poor and lose everything. Word bombs in relation to man's salvation decisions, are cluster bombs, packed with emotions such as fear, doubt, rejection, and other negative impulses. Without proper attention from us, especially you guardians, we cannot guide our charges in making the correct decision.

"There is almost no shortage of negative, destructive word bombs. When we observe these word bombs, we uncover them and expose them to truth. For example, faith is the opposite of fear, hope is the opposite of hopelessness. This might seem rather obvious, but when man cannot see the word bomb, he can only feel its effects. Humans must be vigilant against the enemy's word bombs," Mark warned, "as they prey on the mind's vulnerabilities, seeking to misdirect and control."

We were taken to another scene without even climbing on our light boards. The saboteurs took us to what was like an observation chamber, even though it looked like the same forest we had been standing in. I thought to myself that we were, indeed, in the same place, but possibly in another time.

Mark motioned to a man sitting nearby to us, his shoulders slumped in despair.

"Observe how the bombs have crippled this one," he said. "Doubt and fear are the shackles that bind him, the enemy plants destructive ideas in the human mind, where, like seeds, they take root. They are whispers that breed mistrust, anxiety, or apathy. Or all of those. Once rooted, they overwhelm a person's true thoughts and feelings."

A saboteur drifted over silently and enveloped the troubled man in his cloak. When the cloak floated away, the man's head was raised, his eyes clear.

Mark nodded. "Our cloaks dissolve the word bombs, liberating the captive mind. But humans must also develop their own defences." He met my gaze. "When a man is facing difficult choices, be wary of doubts that foster his paralysis. At the cliff's edge, your job is to help him ignore the trembling fear of falling. And when pursuing life's purpose, you are there to assist him in dismissing the voice that says his dreams are futile. When faced with an important life decision, say, like choosing a career path, word bombs of self-doubt and fear of failure may overwhelm a person, causing inaction and despair.

When facing major life decisions," continued Mark, "people are often assailed by doubts and anxieties from the enemy, feelings and thoughts that threaten to paralyse them. Voices in their head sow seeds of inadequacy and fear of failure, convincing them they are unqualified to take the path before them, trapping them in indecision," said Mark. "Negative thoughts create mistrust, isolating people from the Father's community and breaking bonds of friendship between them. When given the opportunity to stand against injustice, a man's courage and conviction can be bombarded with apathy, timidity and excuses for inaction. People often miss the chance to create positive change. Those in power can be tempted by greed and have their priorities twisted, leading to unethical behaviour. The enemy uses this to tempt people into corruption.

CHAPTER 11

"Bombardments of helplessness and weakness will tempt a man to surrender to cravings that sustain addictions and harmful habits."

I felt sorry for the human beings. How much I wanted to help protect them from violent word bombs, assaulting their identity and self-care with unworthiness and self-loathing. When they were in states of grief.

Mark pointed out; the voice of despair muffled their need to reach out, and trapped a human being in a refusal to heal. Mark said that the enemy tailors these attacks to each person's vulnerabilities. But, he said, by recognising the source of these word bombs, we angels can help a person to dismantle them. With truth on our side, we could help a man reclaim his true thoughts and so help him live up to his full potential.

"We protect people when they're under attack and they call for help from the Father," concluded Mark. "Our role is to be a barrier between the person and the enemy, intercepting any attacks and following the Father's guidance."

"Thank you, Mark, for explaining to these young guardians what you do," said Mac. "I'm sure as they begin to work with you and you with them, you will both learn a lot from the saboteurs," he said, turning to Seymour and me.

"Now we are going on a new exercise," Mac's voice slowed down, indicating that this would not be just fun and games. "This time," he said, "we are going deep into enemy territory. The saboteurs will accompany us, and you will see first-hand how effective they are and how important it is that we angels work together as one unit."

"Are we also going to go?" I asked, feeling both excited and agitated.

"Yes, Shiloh, you and Seymour will be at my side, as I want you to observe the enemy up close," said Mac.

"I am sure we will be fine and that we have nothing to fear," said Seymour, with his usual grin.

"Okay, I have faith, and I believe that we can learn to enjoy our contacts with the enemy," I said.

"Right, Herman," Mac said, without another moment's hesitation, "I want you to give these guardians some weapons. A sword each and then they can choose between the net or the crossbow."

A blanket appeared in front of us. Herman bent down, undid the buckle and rolled it out. There were many weapons of varied sizes and shapes, all seated in pockets.

Herman stood back and motioned to us to choose our weapons.

One sword stood out to me as a good size, not too large, with a comfortable-looking handle, and a protective guard around the shield, with gold and silver shapes that moved constantly. It spoke to me; it almost sang to me. A hum flowed over me, and I heard it say, "I'm the one." I reached down and picked it up, and I could hear a communal grunt of approval from the warriors. I placed the sword at my side and tightened the buckle. It fitted comfortably, becoming a natural part of me.

Seymour bent down and picked up a curved sword. Its tip was quite wide and almost had a hook on the end. It was double-edged and is sharp indeed. His sword did not have a hilt but had a golden clip. The sword attached itself to the belt blade and changed from invisible to visible at his command. It also looked dull, or shiny. He took great pleasure in showing me how he knew he could control it.

Then I looked at a net, which was rolled into a tight ball in one of the pockets in the blanket. I wondered why we would ever want a net. I reached down and grabbed it, and it opened in front of me. I knew how to control it. All I had to do was look where it needed to go, and it would wrap itself around the object. I knew intuitively that I needed to choose it. So I did.

Seymour reached down and grabbed a crossbow and also picked up a quiver full of arrows. They were short and stubby and had different arrowheads. I looked, and I could see words were written on the shaft. One read Truth, another Faith, and another Hope.

"Well, it looks like we are ready, Shiloh," Mac said, sounding pleased. "Garrick, you will accompany Shiloh and teach him the finer details of how to track and look for signs."

Garrick was one of the saboteurs. He was a bit smaller than Mark and a lot nimbler. He carried a bow and a sword and was alert to his surroundings. His cloak pulsated as he walked, it moved out to the sides and behind them and then withdrew back into his mantle.

"Herman, I want you to lead the way,". Mark to the bowman, "We will follow you at a short distance. Garrick, you are to accompany Herman and alert us to any traps the enemy might have set."

I followed Herman, staying close by Garrick. His eyes were alert to the path in front of us. He observed everything, from the grass to the branches of the trees and the animals and birds.

"Shiloh, you need to observe your surroundings," he said. "Birds and animals, by their very nature, need to be observant and they alert you to any danger. Even if they can't always see our realm, their senses are accurate. The enemy is restricted because of who he is," he went on. "He may not pass from man's realm to the Father's realm. He is imprisoned in his own realm but has access to man's realm. They are interconnected, just as ours is with man."

Soon, Garrick spotted something in the grass. He pointed at it, and I saw that it was lying still and camouflaged. It was curled up and seemed to be waiting for something. It was long, legless, and had a diamond-shaped head with a tongue that shot in and out. Its eyes were bright yellow with slits of black. It saw us and raised itself up slowly and made a puffing noise, followed by a hiss. Garrick motioned to us to give it a wide berth. He proceeded to tell us that this was called a snake and was not there to harm us.

"However," he told me, "the enemy does use them to harm man. The enemy will place them in the path of man, so that the snake, in its own defence, might attack man and, sometimes out of aggression or fear, the snake will bite a man, causing great deal of pain and sometimes death, if the bite is not treated in time. In this way, the enemy achieves his work without revealing himself to man. Man ends up blaming the animal," he said.

We continued on the path down the mountain slope until we saw wisps of smoke in the distance.

"The smoke is a sign of man's presence," said Mark, who had been following close behind us. "Man uses fire for many things. One of them is cooking. Man takes meat from birds or animals and puts it into the fire. By doing this, he cooks the meat and then eats it. He also uses fire to clear the land, so that he might build a house or prepare a field for planting. The fire burns hot and consumes wood and scrub and grass. Fire is important to man. It keeps him warm when it is cold. Understand, we do not feel the cold or the heat. We are not subject to many of the physical boundaries of man's world. Sadly, the enemy often uses fire to destroy man's work. In this way, the enemy makes man's life difficult."

As we got closer to where the smoke was coming from, we could hear chattering and laughter coming what turned out to be an entire village. There must have been about 15 children playing in the dirt as they kicked a ball around, shouting in excitement as one kicked a round object. The others would chase it, some giggling, others shouting.

The atmosphere was one of happiness and they were loving their game. I later learned that the round object was part of the inside of the animal. It was called the bladder, and when blown up with air from their mouths, then sealed and dried it in the sun, and it became an object of fun.

A group of older men were sitting underneath the tree chatting and laughing. Women, who all looked a little like Eve, rather than like Adam, were busy around the small fires.

They had long sticks, which protruded out of big black pots that sat on top of the fires. They seem to be stirring substances in the pots with the sticks.

As I watched, Mark noticed and commented, "They are stirring their food in those black pots. The fire is heating up the food and cooking it."

As we watched and observed the villagers going about their daily tasks, Garrick and Mac went on ahead. They disappeared from our vision. Herman ordered us to activate our vests, so that we would be invisible to the enemy. I felt proud to be using this vital piece of equipment I'd earned. As I activated it, it grew longer and wider, matching my cloak, hiding my sword and net completely.

Then Mac returned. He approached Herman and said, "There's a group hanging around the witchdoctor's hut."

"Go, warriors, be on the alert, as they are bound to have their guards placed around the hut. Mark, Herman, join Garrick, I want you to go ahead and check the traps. Shiloh and Seymour, stay at my side," he ordered.

The two bowmen and the saboteur angel moved ahead and then vanished under the cover of their cloaks. Our own cloaks were firmly buckled, and I felt safe and secure, knowing that neither the men nor the enemy could see us.

The children continued to play, and the women were not aware of us passing them by. I peered into one of the black pots, a thick white substance was been stirred. It bubbled and gave off little puffs of steam as it cooked over the fire. The women were chatting amongst each other, laughing, and sometimes using a clicking sound as part of their language.

We continued towards the witchdoctor's hut. It was placed further out from the rest of the villager's huts. It had a ring of old, sun-bleached logs surrounding it, forming a protective barrier. There was an open entrance with an archway, and on top of the arch was a sun-bleached goat's skull.

"Shiloh, this is a sign of the enemy's realm," Mac explained, "showing us that the witchdoctor is one of his servants. The witchdoctor works for the enemy and against his own people. For a long time now, villagers here have not been pleased with this witchdoctor, as he is using the power given to him by the enemy to his own advantage, rather than helping the villagers. These villagers have been calling upon the Father to come and help them get rid of this witchdoctor and his power that hangs over them and controls them."

"Why would a witchdoctor, being a man, side with the enemy? I don't understand how he thinks it will help him," I asked.

CHAPTER 11

"Shiloh, power can be a destructive force that seems to govern much of what is going on in man's realm," Mac replied.

We joined Mark and Herman and stood in a semicircle outside the boundaries of the hut and waited for Mac, Garrick and the other saboteurs to do the search. They found many things in the ground that were strategically placed around the hut to protect the witchdoctor.

As we waited, scanning the dimly lit archway to the compound, a raucous band of creatures came into view.

They were divided into three unruly clusters, numbering about eleven in total. Nearest to us was a trio tasked with guarding the entrance.

The largest of the bunch was an ugly brute, his warty green skin sagging in folds around his scowling face. With every jerk of his head, ropes of slimy drool went flying. His armour ancient, patches of rust spreading like a disease across the battered iron shoulder plates. They creaked and groaned with his every movement. Around his waist he wore studded leather, the sharp spikes glinting dangerously in the flickering torchlight. He looked eager for a fight, as did his compatriots.

The rest of the chaotic crew seemed caught up in their own unseemly conversations, oblivious to our quiet presence ... for now. We would have to tread carefully to avoid detection by these unfriendly forces.

Suddenly, the wretched creatures became aware of our presence and sprang to attention. The gnarled, grey-skinned beasts drew their jagged swords, baring yellow fangs in savage snarls. Crouching, their bloodshot eyes darted about wildly in search of the unseen threat.

Arrows whistled through the darkness, finding their marks with sickening thuds. Two of the gangly creatures let out agonised howls as arrows pierced their flesh, knocking them off their feet, and they fell onto the hard stone floor. The others reacted quickly, raising their dented shields just in time to deflect the next volley.

Our bowmen closed in, encircling the vile beasts as they cowered behind their shields, realising they were outmatched. Herman commanded them to be bound and banished from the place at once. Fiery tendrils like living snakes wrapped around each writhing creature, binding them individually and together in a fiery bundle. The flames licked their rough hide without burning, yet it instilled mortal terror in their simple minds. More afraid of failing their master than of us, they whimpered and struggled, but to no avail. Our enemy was captured, and this innocent place was made safe once more.

The witchdoctor emerged from his hut, draped in the speckled fur of a leopard skin. The creature's onyx and amber pelt was wrapped around his hunched shoulders, its long, elegant tail dangling across his wrinkled forehead. "Where are you?" he cried out, searching in vain for his demonic masters. "Why have you abandoned me?" The old man's voice cracked with desperation. "You cannot forsake me! You swore I would be protected!"

He staggered forward, eyes wide with disbelief that he had been left defenceless. The witchdoctor continued to call out in anguish to the powers that had manipulated him, promising prestige and influence in exchange for his sinister services. But, struck by the perilous arrows of the bowmen, they had been captured and had left their trusting servant to his fate. Now, stripped of the otherworldly aids that had elevated him, the frail old man seemed small and pitiable, nothing more than a pawn that had outlived its usefulness.

Herman allowed himself to appear to the witchdoctor and spoke, "You will never call upon these evil powers again to gain control over your people. From now on, you will not be the witchdoctor of this community. We have removed your helpers, and they will not have authority here. These people have called upon the Father for help, and He has honoured their faith in Him."

The witchdoctor was trembling and fell on his knees and called out to Herman.

"Please have mercy on me. I did not understand what I was doing. Please do not harm me. I can now see that you're more powerful than they were."

"You will go to the chief of this village and explain to him what has happened to you today and what it means for the village, now that they are free to worship the real Father. The Father, in return, will forgive you if you ask Him – so long as you never fall back into old ways! All your curses are now lifted and have no effect on these people anymore. If you ask for mercy and forgiveness, the Father grants this. You will be free as well."

My sword was still in its scabbard, but my hand was on the handle. I was not sure what I'd even do if I had to draw the sword, but its presence comforted me. Seymour, on the other hand, was right up there with the Herman, sword drawn and ready to wield its awesome power.

As the witchdoctor walked off to explain himself to the chief, Herman turned to me and said, "Seymour sometimes thinks he's more warrior than guardian."

We looked around to see much more joy in the village. The men had gathered outside a large hut in the centre of the village, which the witchdoctor had entered. The chief came out and greeted the men with a smile. Next to him was the witchdoctor, his head hung low, and his shoulders sagged.

"Today, our Father has sent us much help," the chief declared, "and He has rid us of the affliction of the demons. The power that they have held over this village has been removed and has also been taken away from this witchdoctor. From today, you will be known as a simple herbalist," he said to the witchdoctor. "His knowledge of healing through plants will still be valuable to us as a tribe," the chief told his villagers, "and he assures me he will not entertain and work for the demons again."

With that, a loud cheer rose from the crowd, and they began to dance. Out came big round drums and their rhythmic thump echoed across the land. The women made strange noises with their tongues and voices – sort of a bird sound, full of joy, triumphant. We watched them for a while as they danced around and around, drums beating and women ululating.

Untainted joy had returned to the village. Even the children had stopped playing with their ball and joined in with the dancing. They made their hearts known to the Father and gave Him the glory. We could sense that, because the truth from the hearts seemed to rise towards the curtain that separated their realm from ours.

Even though we had the victory, the saboteurs never let their guard down. They were still watching and being observant of everything. But my mentor Seymour could not contain himself and ran ahead into the crowd of women and children and started to dance with them. They, of course, could not see him, but that did not bother him. He lifted his arms in the air and jumped and twisted and somersaulted over their heads. He was laughing and enjoying the moment. Herman looked on and grinned.

"Aren't you going to go join them, Shiloh, go on, go and try to dance, we will enjoy the spectacle."

I walked over to the group and, as I drew closer, waves of their music washed over me in light colours – not as intense as in our realm, but still beautiful, I realised I needed to take the time to look and feel. There was a power behind the music. I tried to let myself go and wave my arms around awkwardly and tried to kick my legs up like Seymour did, but it just did not feel right. Well, not as right as he made it look, but it was good to see the smiles on the faces of the children and women. There was real joy in their faces, their eyes were shining, and their white teeth glistened in the sunlight. It felt good to be so close among humans – which is vital for us guardians. I understood why Herman had encouraged me

We gathered and returned home. The saboteurs went ahead and checked out our path. Seymour was excitedly chatting to Herman about how wonderful it felt to dance with man.

We arrived at the curtain and returned our extra weapons. We had not need to use them, which Mark said was no bad thing – rather safe than sorry. Then Herman said to me, "You lead the way, Shiloh."

As we passed through the curtain, colours dazzled us, the sounds and smells, everything intensified, and I felt relieved as I knew I was home. We wandered down to a clearing.

"Well, bowmen," said Mark, "I want you to share a full report of what arrows you shot and why. I want to know what you were thinking and what you perceived the enemy was thinking when we attacked. And Seymour and Shiloh, you can also tell me what you felt when the attack happened."

I pondered the question. One thing was for sure, we were on the winning team. I had no doubts that we would beat the enemy. The only thing I was concerned about was what if I were on my own and not with the bowmen and the saboteurs?

"Shiloh, you're never alone," Seymour reminded me, and Mac and Mark joined in, both echoing each other: "You guardians are just a call away, and we will be with you. We have been assigned to you. We are your hosts and helpers."

I must say, it felt good to know that whenever I went on an assignment, I would have this team of amazing bowmen and saboteurs taking care of me and I knew they would help me to take care of man.

Chapter 12

Shields United

We had hardly left the clearing, or so it felt, when Seymour spoke.

"Shiloh," he said, "The bowmen are here again, and they want us to accompany them. Are you ready, are you coming?"

I looked at Seymour and said, "Why, where are we going this time?"

Although the experiences of the past few days had been overwhelming for me, expectancy rose in my belly at once, it was that feeling of excitement again. "Are we going off grid again?" I asked.

Seymour seemed to be far off. Something preoccupied him, which did not shock me. He was, I saw, communicating with the bowmen. Then he suddenly interrupted himself and shouted, "Come on, Shiloh, we haven't got all day, you know!"

"Hey, I'm ready!" I retorted, amazing myself with my energy. The knowledge that we were all working together was evidently giving me far more strength than I'd ever known I could have.

"Excellent," replied Seymour, putting his arm around my shoulder, and we walked towards the group of bowmen, standing and waiting, but also in deep discussion about something.

We arrived and nodded our greetings. There was a sense of urgency among them, and Herman said, "You two, are you up for another trip?"

"Yes, we are definitely up for another trip," I said.

Seymour grinned and remarked that I had come a long way from being young. Hmmm, I thought, maybe I have – I have developed a taste for adventure. Suddenly, I felt the presence of the saboteurs. I knew they would be around and so when Mac and Garrick appeared out of nowhere, I was not surprised.

Mark gave us a briefing. "The young girl, whom we are planning to help, has been under the influence of the enemies. Her mother is not sure what is wrong with her daughter, but she has called out to the Father for help.

"The girl's guardian angels, Basra and Kalu, need us to team up with them," he went on. Basra is a formidable guardian angel," he informed us, "gifted at anticipating and evading the traps set by the enemy forces trying to harm his young charge. He has centuries of experience and knows how to counter threats, his sword and shield are always at the ready.

"Kalu, Basra's protégé, has the role of gently escorting their charge, keeping her free of injury. They form an unshakeable team, but today they need our help," Mark concluded.

"It will be good to see guardians in action," I confided in Seymour, whose arm had lain reassuringly around my shoulder throughout Mark's briefing.

"Right Herman, could you hand out the weapons please?" Mac commanded, his authoritative voice cutting through the air.

Swish! With a practiced motion, Herman directed the bundle of weapons towards us. It swung into our view and rolled out across the ground, almost as eager to rid itself of its arsenal as we were to accept the goods. The various blades and implements glinted in the light, a deadly array of angelic armaments.

I received my favorite sword, its familiar weight settling comfortably in my hand, along with my trusty net. But there was an additional weapon I didn't recognize at first. It was rolled up as small as a fist, intriguing in its compact form. As I reached out to take it, curiosity piqued, it suddenly unravelled before my eyes. The weapon revealed itself as four gleaming metallic balls, each one attached at the end of a fiery rope that crackled with ethereal energy. I marveled at its unique design, wondering how it would fare in the coming battle.

I glanced at Garrick, who just winked and said, "It will serve you well Shiloh." I knew it was one of the special items the saboteurs used to bind up the enemy – like they had bound the entities that served the witchdoctor. Maybe I would even have opportunity to use it, and my sword or net, on this trip.

CHAPTER 12

The rest of the group picked out their weapons and made sure they were well prepped for the task at hand.

"We will go in as a team. I want you two guardians to be with me," said Mac, his voice carrying a weight of authority. He paused, his eyes scanning our faces before continuing. "We had a great trip last time to sort out the witchdoctor, but this is different. This mission presents unique challenges we must be prepared for. I want you to observe the many different layers of attack that the enemy uses. Pay close attention to their tactics and strategies. And I'm sure you will pick up what needs to be done when we encounter the enemy. Your instincts and training will guide you but stay alert and adaptable. This experience will be invaluable for your growth as guardians."

The group gathered and headed to the entrance of the curtained gateway. Mac went through first, followed by the saboteurs and then the bowmen and, of course, us two guardians.

We arrived on top of a hill with some enormous oak trees and a worn path that led to an open area. The air was crisp. The sun was still up, but receding to the horizon. I looked around, and there was our commission about fifty yards away. A rambling town, not big, was spread out below the hill and small houses were dotted about, surrounded by open, well-tended fields. I could see a few people working in the fields and walking on the various roads. it looked like a normal afternoon on earth at first sight, but we knew all was not right here on the hill.

A young girl was sitting on a wooden bench overlooking the town. She was weeping. Her hands were stretched out on her lap as she was mumbling to herself between the sobs. All around her were horrible, nasty-looking entities, whispering and shouting in her ear.

I heard one of them say, "You can do it. Go on deeper, it will make you feel alive and release all the pain."

In the one corner was a dark, big, threatening-looking entity, who seemed to be giving out the commands. The saboteurs moved to one side, and there was another group of entities who were coming in to try to increase their numbers. The bowmen intercepted them, and they fled. I felt their arrows fly past me.

Seymour said, "Put your cloak on, make sure you have activated the vest too, as this is going to be an interesting clash."

I pressed the spot in the front of the vest that activated its ability to deflect arrows.

We watched as the bowmen moved in, shooting their bows as we moved. They took the enemy unawares, and arrows hit. We could hear the thumps and the whooshing of their arrows as they flew to find their targets.

While this was all going on, the young girl on the bench seemed oblivious. She sat staring at her arms on her lap. The knife that she had used was lying on the ground, covered in blood. Blood ran down her forearms into her hands and then dripped onto the ground, where the blood, which was starting to congeal, had attracted masses of ants and flies. Her two guardians, Basra, and Kula wore grieved expressions on their faces, but they were aware that much-needed help had arrived.

Saboteurs set traps in four separate places and lay in wait as the bowmen steered the enemy towards them. The large entity was shouting and screaming his orders, but by now his horde was on the run. There were a few persistent entities who were now in a frenzy from the smell of blood and their great success. They were whispering into her ear.

"You can do it, do it again, this time cut deeper, cut the other way so that you bleed more and release more pain, you will feel much better when it is done, go on, cut your skin."

The other one said, "Your parents don't love you and have abandoned you, you can come with us. We will take care of you; we will look after you."

Even though the girl could not see them, she understood them at some level. She must have heard the voices of thought she had, and she obeyed what they were saying, as if she was under a spell or power. I understood, with a sense of deep grief, that the entities had managed to block off the voices of her guardians.

The saboteurs slipped into the shadows, laying traps for the enemy. Arrows whistled past as the bowmen aimed at the shadowy horde. Cries of fury and pain erupted as arrows found their marks. But the largest shadow, their leader, only laughed. He continued spurring the girl towards further bloodshed. His minions echoed his toxic words, driving her tortured mind.

I rushed forward, desperate to intervene. I was with the warriors now, even though I was a guardian. The girl tensed, knife in hand. My heart dropped as she slashed again at her scarred arm, the shadows cheering her on.

"Stop!" I cried out. "Don't listen to them – this is not the answer!"

Basra and Kula looked at me in amazement. Without hesitation, they echoed my words, persistently clearing a way to reach her heart.

CHAPTER 12

The girl froze, confusion and anguish warring on her face. The shadows screeched in anger at my interference. I knew we had to act fast before they regained control.

Herman moved in. He had his axe unsheathed, swung it violently and hit the one entity across the side of the head. The entity went tumbling down the hill towards one of the bowmen, who promptly threw a set of chains around him and obliged him with a kick to the head.

Another entity looked up in horror, but he was too late. The axe came down and hit him squarely on the chest. Thump. We heard the axe as it slammed into his chest so hard that it exploded the vest the entity had on. It burst the buckles, and the entity somersaulted and landed at the feet of one of the Bowmen, who thrust a spear into his chest, pinning him down. The entity was then bound and thrown on the heap with the others.

The big entity, the leader of the horde, turned his attention to us, as he must have felt we were inexperienced. He came charging at us, head down, but he had dropped his guard as he closed in. I released my net from its pouch and held it up, ready to command it to do my bidding.

Seymour drew his sword and launched himself towards the entity. There was an almighty clash as they hit each other. There was a blinding flash of light as Seymour's sword slammed into the side of the entity and struck the hilt of his undrawn sword. The entity looked horrified as we threw the net over him and pinned him down.

He looked at us through the holes in the net and said, "You are only guardians, how is it possible for you to take on and defeat a mighty lieutenant?"

I looked at the lieutenant and said, "You are not mighty in any way. The least of us will always defeat you."

We threw the lieutenant onto the pile, along with his horde, and the saboteurs removed them from the field of battle.

The girl came to her senses, as if she were waking up from a bad dream. She looked down at her arms and screamed aloud, "Not again! Why do I do this? I must be crazy."

She reached into the bag next to her and pulled out a long piece of cloth, Kula was whispering into her ear thoughts of comfort and of action. Basra was standing guard with a shield and had two bowmen at his side. He was directing the bowman to the positions of the entities trying to attack the girl, and the bowmen dealt with them swiftly. Such teamwork and level-headedness were amazing.

The girl knew instinctively that she had to go back home to her parents and get help. She wrapped her injuries with shaking hands. Then, casting one last horrified look at the bloodied knife, she rose, feeling lightheaded from the loss of blood. She mumbled to herself, "Come on, you can do this," as she summoned all the energy she could muster and stood up. All the while, Kula was whispering encouragement into her ear.

She stumbled but managed to walk down the hill to the village. She left the knife on the bloodied ground, with no intention to return to it. As she walked down the hill, her mind became less foggy, as the traps and arrows from the entities had been overcome by the saboteurs, and two bowmen flanked her for protection. Kula continued to whisper into her mind, and she became visibly stronger, but the toll of her ordeal had been immense.

She arrived at a thatched cottage that had a lovely garden full of roses in full bloom. The fragrance of the roses filled the air. She pushed the wooden gate open and walked underneath the arch that formed a framework for a red climbing rose. The stone pathway to the house was short, but to her I could see it was an endless journey. She knew that she needed help. I could feel her dread the embarrassment and the questions that would soon come.

Then her mother was out of the door, her mouth opened wide with shock and horror. She ran to her daughter and took her in her arms and carried her into the house. She called out to her husband to fetch a doctor. The father looked at his daughter with fear and dread. He was very close to her and loved her, but at this moment he felt confused, betrayed, and terrified that he would lose her.

I saw him run as fast as he could down the road. A strange blue object made a loud noise as he ran in front of it. I was later to learn that it was known as a car and that people travelled inside the car, just like we travelled on the light board, to get to places faster. He ran up to the blue car's door and thumped his hand against it as hard as he could several times. The door opened and an elderly man with a great big white moustache and round spectacles that covered his eyes greeted him with an alarmed expression on his face. I heard him say, "Of course, I can be there right now."

The doctor rushed over to the cottage with a small black bag at his side.

The bowmen and the saboteurs were still on duty, searching for any further entities that might want to take advantage of the trauma. We found them trying to influence the girl's family with anger and hurt.

There was a new leader, hunched over, coughing, and grunting as he gave his orders. His companions were vomiting lies over the mom's head and shooting arrows at the girl,

CHAPTER 12

but Seymour and I had our shields up and had called the bowman in. In came the volley of fresh arrows. Two lowly soldiers among the entities were taken down and flung to the ground. Mark threw the fiery rope, and I followed his example, stepped in front of the leader, and released my fiery rope with the four balls. Garrick had been right – this thing would serve me today. Out it flew, with a bolt of light, and ignited around the leader's legs. Down he went, screaming in pain and writhing on the ground. Garrick stepped over, winked at me, and bound them together. Then they were sent off with the rest.

I noted something that day – the enemy might lose the battle on one front but is always starting another. They had lost on the hill and then tried to gain a foothold in the cottage by spreading hatred and fear amongst the girl's parents and family. They look for an angle to influence man negatively. All the angels, us guardians, the saboteurs, and the bowmen were on alert. We had cleared each area of the enemy, but even so, we needed to remain on guard.

The doctor attended to the girl. He had stopped the bleeding and bandaged her arms. She lay on the bed, her mother speaking to her, trying to reassure her that everything would be okay.

Her father was pacing up and down, muttering to himself. Standing at the window, looking out of the house over his lovely rose garden, he could not understand why his daughter, to whom he had given so much, who had such a comfortable life, would take such a drastic step to end it.

Mark came swiftly up besides the father and wrapped his clock around him, the father took a breath and relaxed the anxiety left him and the worry and fear of losing his daughter vanished as the cloak removed all of them and Mark slipped away. the father looked over at his daughter and floods of emotion and relief and love filled the air around him, waves of love flowed over the bed and lay on his daughter.

Herman walked over to us as we looked at the scene and said,

"Now, you two. Did you observe how relentless the enemy is? Even though he was beaten on the hill, he made havoc here at the cottage. Never underestimate what he can do, his only interest is to destroy. But if you understand your enemy and how he thinks," he continued, "you stand a good chance of out-witting him – just as we have done today. You both did well today. However, next time, try not to get too involved, as I don't want Ralph to fear for your well-being on these trips. Like yourselves, he was also involved when he went on missions, so he does understand the reasons why you do it, but he also understands the danger."

The other bowmen had gathered in a group. They were comparing notes on various aspects of the confrontation. They shared how close they had been to getting beaten, yet they triumphed.

Then Mark instructed them to get ready as they were going on another mission. Already! Did they never pause? Mark turned to us and said, "Thank you for coming along and thank you for your help. You need to head up to portal seven again. I'm sure Ralph has a lesson for you. You can tell your class what you have learnt today. Remember, the enemy is always looking for a gap."

Without another word, we moved towards the gateway, parted the curtain, and found our light boards were waiting for us. We mounted our boards and soared upward, heading back to our realm.

Chapter 13

Strongholds of Abuse Shattered

The Great Hall towered above us, pillars of marble stretching up into the vaulted ceilings far overhead. I never tired of the intricate carvings adorning each pillar with scenes of myth and legend etched into the stone. Seymour and I walked over the polished floors, past the giant screens displaying ancient scenes. Some screens sometimes swirled and left their pillars, to wrap themselves around other pillars and display their wonders to the young students.

At the centre of the hall today stood a magnificent table, looking as if it has been carved from a single, ancient oak tree. Its surface was covered with a chaos of scrolls, books, and strange instruments. A handful of teachers sat hunched over the clutter, white robes spilling over the bench seats, their voices an inaudible murmur. One looked up at our approach, eyes glinting sharply from beneath a tangle of braided beard.

"Seymour, Shiloh," he called, beckoning us with a crooked finger. The other teachers glanced up with mild interest. "We have an errand for you. Seek out Ralph in his study upstairs."

Seymour shot me a knowing grin, then sprang into the air as if gravity held no sway over him. I hurried to follow, bounding upward through the open space. Four floors up we alighted on a balcony that encircled the hall. Down below, the table and its occupiers had shrunk to a hazy blur.

We set off down the curving passage, flanked by doors leading into lecture halls and portal rooms. I stayed close on Seymour's heels, until, at last we came to an arched wooden door, bearing Ralph's seal. Within, we found him conversing with another teacher in hushed tones. They broke off at our entrance, faces creasing into smiles.

The teachers grinned. Ralph's colleague was tall, with a long, braided white beard, which he stroked, eyeing us out with a probing, quizzical look.

"Well! Seymour, I see you have a willing accomplice!"

He gestured in my direction. We stood awkwardly, waiting for the reason for our summons to be made known

Smiling at us, he continued. "Ralph and I have been discussing your recent adventures on earth – adventures, which have been a vital part of training. We feel you two should go on a trip to see another side of your work." He paused. "Seymour, you know what we are talking about, but Shiloh – you have earned the privilege of seeing that part of your job that is the most rewarding."

Speaking in a commanding, yet soft voice, he informed us that Kalu and Basra had asked for us, because something interesting was happening.

"Basra gave me a detailed report on your last exploit, which I have handed to Ralph, who will discuss it with you. And may I say, Shiloh, you are becoming more like Seymour by the day."

With that, he chuckled, tapped Ralph on the shoulder, and vanished.

"Well, now," Ralph chuckled. He explained that we were to aid the two guardians, who were senior students, namely, Kalu and Basra. They were observing something extraordinary unfold.

My curiosity was piqued. What marvels would we witness? Bidding our teacher farewell, we set off, ready for our next adventure.

"Let's go through portal five," Seymour suggested. "Shiloh, you have not experienced it yet, as it is usually reserved it for urgent incursions. Our visit today can hardly be called an 'incursion', but we are here to practise, hey!"

We moved towards portal five, a small opening between two enormous oak trees that guarded the entrance. This portal was for emergency chutes, which transport you immediately to a place of trouble. It would be my first time down this portal, and I had a sense that it would shoot us straight down like fireballs. Not the luxury of riding on my Humba, I thought.

Seymour looked at me and smiled.

"No need for Humba. Just bring your light board, and let's go. We will fly fast, and this time you must lie on the board. Do not stand on it. We want to be quick. As you get down to the bottom, you need to pull up the front, and you will do a few somersaults and land. You get everything on first go anyway, Shiloh, so I wouldn't worry."

"Oh yes – one more thing," he said, "the lights will pass us in streaks as time itself will be warped. We will get a hop into the loop, as it is known. Dive into the column, and as the change of colour occurs, the loop of time is dissected and inverted. You will pass through a loop in time and be where you desire to be. Keep your mind focused on where you want to end up, or else you will end up in the wrong place!"

Trembling with anticipation, I followed Seymour. As we hopped into the loop, the bright colours flooded all over us and swirled and flashed we seemed to go down a twisting shaft and it rushed past us. I stayed close to Seymour, as I did not want to end up in another time zone alone. It was like the time we went down the cliff-face of ferns, but this time there were neither ferns nor a sloping cliff-face, this time, there was just air. We went straight down and went into man's realm in an instant. Numerous colours came whizzing past me, and I tumbled.

I heard Seymour say, "Just relax, keep your head down, point down, the board knows what to do and I will give you fair warning when you need to pull up the front."

Down we shot, the scenery was blurred, not because of the air in my eyes, but because of the immense speed at which we travelled. We were flying close to the ground, mountains flashed past, and we could see forests rolling on for miles, big giant trees swaying in the wind as we rushed by. The Earth came up at me at a terrific speed. We saw the girl who had tried to end her life sitting on a bench with her mother, the exact place where she had almost taken her own life. They were talking.

Seymour said, "Pull up. Okay, Shiloh, pull-up, hard now!"

I pulled the nose up harder, and the board took me into three somersaults, rolled in and Seymour shouted, "Release your wings!"

"What?"

"Release your wings!"

"How?" I replied.

In the next instant, my wings released themselves. They came out from inside my back, flapped around the side and came to an abrupt stop, hovering over the girl. She felt the wind. I looked at Seymour and said, "Look! She felt the wind, she felt our wings."

"Yes, Shiloh," smiled Seymour proudly, "that is one thing, one of many things we can do to reveal our presence. We can playfully reveal our presence by moving our charges' belongings, or even by leaving a distinct scent."

He looked at me with a glint in his eye. "Only pleasant ones, mind you. The souls sometimes detect the enemy by an odour, and he does not smell nice at all!"

Basra and Kula welcomed us with broad grins.

"Thanks for coming again, Shiloh. We felt it important for you to see all sides of our task of caring for our charges. It's not all battle and gore," said Basra.

As we chatted, the girl looked up and around, taking in the beautiful scenery, the trees in autumn, the leaves turning red and yellow gold. There was a slight, not unpleasant chill in the air.

She snuggled into her mother's side and said, "Mum, thank you, thank you for standing by me. Thank you for helping me."

Her mother looked at her, squeezed her and replied. "I'll do anything for you, Carol, anything at all. But remember this. The Lord heard my prayers, and He sent an army of angels to save you that day."

"I know!" Carol replied. "I can feel they are with us right now."

On hearing her words, we guardians all beamed at each other.

"All you have to do is ask the Lord to show you," replied her mother.

Seymour flapped his left wing across the front of them. They looked at each other, knowing someone was listening, and the mother smiled.

"I think it's an angel just saying hello," she mused happily. Then she continued. "Carol, I sense the deep hurt and turmoil you experienced after what happened with your uncle. As your mother, I ache for the pain you have endured. What he did was terribly wrong – the responsibility lies fully with him, not with you. You did nothing to encourage or deserve his abusive behaviour. "I know you may feel confused and conflicted – it's normal to struggle with complex emotions when someone you trusted betrays you like he did. But please know that you are not to blame. You are still the beautiful, innocent girl I have always known."

She turned to face her daughter straight-on and took her hands in her own. "The cutting worries me deeply, as I know you are trying desperately to cope with overwhelming feelings. I understand the urge to release the pain through physical means. I – " she hesitated, but then went on. "Yes. I, too, resorted to self-harm many years ago, when I felt lost and alone." A tear rolled down her cheek and her daughter put her head onto the mother's shoulder and wept too.

CHAPTER 13

"I learned," said the mother, caressing Carol and containing her own emotion. "Inflicting harm on yourself will not take away the actual pain. Please let's work together to find healthier ways for you to heal?"

Carol lifted her head off her mother's shoulder and looked deeply into her eyes. "Thank you," she breathed, still sniffing.

"My dear child, as your mother, I want you to know that you can always come to me. Never feel you have to hide your feelings or struggle with dark thoughts alone. Bringing things into the light takes away their power – it makes them shrink. Keeping things bottled up allows them to fester and grow out of proportion in our minds.

"When we speak openly about our pain, it loses its grip over us. Sharing with someone we trust can help us gain perspective. Things often seem less scary when we voice them.

"You see, the Father designed family as a refuge, especially the bond between parents and children. That closeness allows healing. Therefore, the enemy tries so hard to divide families – even over minor disagreements. He knows that united, we are strong. But alone, we can lose sight of truth.

"Please know that no matter what you are going through, you have me right by your side. We will walk this road together. My arms will always be open when you need support or a listening ear. You are so loved, my child. We are in this together."

"When uncle Jimmy crossed that line," Carol began crying again. "Mum, I didn't know what to do. He told me that if I told any of you, he would make out that it was me, that I had done it."

"Oh, I know, Carol. That was a poisonous seed, sown by the enemy. Uncle Jimmy is going to have to answer to the Father for what he did. I'm so terribly sorry I never picked up on it earlier. But you can go to the Father and ask Him to cleanse you of all that hurt and pain and abuse.

"Because, you know, He was there with you. While it was all happening, His Son would have been right beside you and looking after you, protecting you. Even though the abuse happened, and Uncle Jimmy crossed that line and invaded your space and took advantage of you. And you were only eight years old!"

The mother sobbed for a few seconds, then gathered herself again as the daughter spoke again.

"I thought it was my fault," Carol said. "Because I was wearing a nightie, and he blamed me. He said, because you are wearing this stuff, because you are innocent, because you are pretty, because ... I used to lie awake at night and sob and cry and wonder where is this God I'm supposed to believe in."

"You know, the same thing happened to me," Carol's mother said. "I was only nine when Uncle Jack started touching me in ways he shouldn't have. He would make me do stuff I didn't want to do. It made me feel gross inside. He kept doing it for three whole years, until I got big enough to make him stop. But even after he stopped, I still felt dirty and ashamed. So, I started cutting myself, to try to get all the bad feelings out. I just wanted the voices in my head to stop telling me I was worthless. I was so desperate. Grandma prayed for me, and that was the only thing that helped."

"So, we both got hurt by someone bad," Carol said, weeping softly again. "But, praying, and talking to people who care helped us both, Mom! I'll always remember how scary it was, though. There are other kids out there, probably, going through the same thing. We should try to help them. We can't let the bad guys win."

The mother retorted said, "Before you think about helping others, you need to do the bravest thing. You have to forgive Uncle Jimmy."

"I am not sure I could ever forgive him, Mom. But with God's help, I could at least try. One day, soon, I promise. For now, I am just so glad the nightmare is over."

A silence fell over the two as they sat on that wooden bench. I looked around, and yes, as I had sensed, many more were watching the scene from a few feet away. They were trying to hide themselves from us, but they were not that good at concealing themselves. Their overzealous attitude allowed their cloaks to drop. The atmosphere had changed, threatening an electric storm.

The mother's guardians were ready to pounce, and Kalu and Basra were poised to attack the entities, in order to protect their charges. Kalu murmured directly into Carol's heart, "You can forgive your uncle, because this will free your soul into your Father's care."

Seymour and I echoed Kalu's words, and Basra flapped his wings.

"You can do it," we hummed in unison.

"Yes," cried Carol softly, grabbing her mother's arm. "I don't want him to have any hold on me ever again. If I forgive him, then God will free me of him! So I do! I forgive you, Uncle Jimmy! I forgive you!" She leapt to her feet and danced a victory dance. "I'm free at last, I'm free!"

As she leapt about in joy, the looming clouds lifted and a fresh breeze blew away all danger, as we angels gently flapped our wings, radiant with joy over their triumph.

CHAPTER 13

The enemy entities shrank back in horror. They no longer had any legal hold over the girl, they were utterly defeated and had to go back to their master in shame and defeat. Bickering and snapping at each other, they slunk off fading away, their snapping and grumbling vanishing with them.

The girl Carol stood, hands lifted high, sending a broad smile right up to heaven as she breathed in the fresh mountain air.

Seymour roared like a lion and flapped his still protruding wings. The breeze lifted Carol's fringe and revealed shiny blue sparkling eyes that had concealed themselves for so long. Yes, she was free at last.

We watched as mother and daughter danced in victory. The smell of freedom really is sweet, I thought.

Basra and Kalu, too, had much reason to celebrate. The victory of the soul is also the guardians' victory. This was sure story for a fireside chat, once they had returned to our heavenly realm. Yes, even we angels long to have a story to tell at the fireside. Away from our home and school, we do not boast or puff ourselves up, but give the Father all the glory. But we all felt great, Carol and her mom and the guardians. The victory empowered us all.

Silently bidding the celebrating family farewell, we slipped back through the forest into the portal's embrace. The mission had deepened my conviction that, no matter what battles loomed, ultimate victory was assured for those who persevered.

Chapter 14

Simple Faith Moves Mountains

On Ralph's express encouragement to witness the perseverance of faith in practice, we returned a third time, to check on the mother and her daughter Carol, and the fields had undergone a transformative impact at the hands of man.

At different strategic locations within the fields, towering stacks of square bales, almost resembling houses, had been placed. The trees were changing their hues, transitioning from green to bolder shades of red and yellow. As we approached the weathered homestead, Seymour told me to picture the pioneering human ancestors, who had carved a living from this hardy soil. Approaching the split-rail fence encircling a chicken run, we inhaled the earthy scent of hay mingled with wood smoke.

The temperature had dropped, showing the onset of colder weather. While these changes did not affect us, Seymour said that it was beneficial for us to immerse ourselves in the earthly atmosphere, as it facilitated a deeper connection with our responsibilities.

Contrary to our peaceful and comfortable home, our experiences on earth are more interactive, and our understanding of them is enhanced when, we exposed ourselves to the full range of climate effects and environmental challenges, which our charges are accustomed to enduring.

Seymour and I approached the house and landed on the back porch. Peering through the smudged window, we saw Carol sitting propped up in bed, nested among floral sheets, her face tranquil in the lamplight as she pored over a book. The cozy scene kindled a glow within us.

CHAPTER 14

Seymour motioned to me to study the room's simple décor. The windows were framed by hand-sewn curtains, on the walls hung faded family photos in chipped frames. In another, small room, which Seymour said was a 'pantry', where cooked goods are stored, there were shelves lined with glass jars of preserved produce.

The peace in the entire space felt hard-won after the recent darkness. I couldn't help but notice that there were storm clouds were massing on the horizon, while Carol's mother dozed in a chair in the next room.

"Look how peaceful she is now," I commented to Seymour. "Her act of forgiveness has lifted a weight from her."

He nodded. "Now that she's been forgiven and released from her self-hatred, she's free to find joy in simple things again."

I glanced at the four chimney stacks. "Humans face daily struggles, such as we angels never experience. They have to chop firewood just to stay warm."

"True, Shiloh," Seymour replied. "We don't need to make such practical efforts. Nor do we battle unseen forces, blind to the surrounding warfare."

I shook my head. "I can't imagine enduring such trials to earn the Father's respect. He already loves humanity unconditionally."

"Exactly," said Seymour. "Their hardships only magnify His love and mercy towards them. Consider how the Father forgave this girl for nearly destroying herself. And how her mother's forgiveness helped set her free."

He paused, "Forgiveness is key to surviving this world, Shiloh. It lifts the burden of bitterness and leaves no foothold for the enemy."

I watched the girl turn a page in her book, and her face relaxed. "I see now her forgiveness has given her a freedom," I observed.

Seymour smiled. "Her story opens all eyes to the power of forgiveness. For humans and angels alike."

Suddenly, however, four dark entities passed through the walls and circled the room. One by one, they crouched down, whispering curses and vile thoughts aimed at the young girl. We watched in horror as their poisonous words seemed to take root in her mind. Her eyes flashed with anger as she glanced through the doorway, at her unsuspecting mother.

Sensing the shift, the mother started and looked up with concern. The entities crept closer, continuing their assault. One vomited disgusting words that dripped down the girl's head like ooze.

The mother's guardian angels prompted her to pray. As she began rebuking the attack in Jesus' name, the atmosphere changed. On command from the Father, several saboteur angels swooped in and bound the entities, flinging them against the wall, which caused them to shriek in terror.

The girl looked confused. Her mother had got out of her chair and come through to soothe her, saying, "Keep reading, dear. Those demons won't bother you anymore."

"Did they come back?" asked Carol.

"They tried, but prayer sent them fleeing. Don't worry, the angels have our backs now."

Special carrier angels now arrived and received the bound demons and removed them. A peaceful presence filled the room once more. The girl sighed in relief. "I thought they had returned."

Her mother smiled "As long as we pray and activate our helpers, we're protected. We must stay alert and not be lazy. But know that God is on our side. Nothing gets past Him."

I was amazed by the woman's spiritual attunement.

"How is she so responsive to God?" I asked Seymour.

"It's simple, Shiloh. The more she prays, the more in tune she becomes. She communes with the Father for hours each day. Not just for herself, but for others, too."

"Please remind me how does the prayer of a soul get to our realm and to the Father," I enquired. Well, Ralph was going to tell you this later on, but you are ahead of the game," chuckled Seymour and winked me.

"When a soul makes the decision to follow the Father, he is a new creation in Christ, which means His tiny spark of light in the spirit of man is ignited. It spreads through his blood to every cell in his physical body. The darkness in his physical body, which was lacking in light, becomes engulfed in light."

"Ah, they are like us – for we are light, are we not?" I exclaimed.

"Well," replied Seymour, "we are light and can take on different forms, but man can only at first be shiny from the inside. They glow at first." We both giggled, when he added, "That's why we sometimes call them glowers.

"They learn to be lighter," he said, "as they pray and read about our realm. Their spirit lives in Jesus They learn how to connect the two parts of themselves – the part that is on earth, and the part that belongs to the Father. And that, dear, young Shiloh, is when they operate from the authority of our realm and the enemy can't touch them."

"Wow, so that means a few people whose spirits are with Jesus can defeat the evil entities," I mused.

"Well, it will need more than a few, but yes, if a man or woman passes the faith onto their sons and daughters as they grow up, yes, they will grow in spiritual authority. But remember Shiloh, the victory is already won. All these souls need to do is to believe and claim the victory of the battle that was already fought and won at the cross. , only a few grasp that. Even so, all can if they chose to, but it is not just a choice they must be active and walk in the belief ."

"Prayer connects humanity to the Father ," he emphasised. "People underestimate their role on Earth. Through prayer, mankind has the final say, not the forces of evil. Their words and faith compel God to act on their behalf. This woman here, Carol's mother, understands the power God has entrusted to her. That's why she prays without ceasing."

I watched the mother and daughter resume their quiet evening, peace enveloping them. What a marvellous example of a human prayer–warrior this mother was!

"One of the first things the lovers of Jesus learned," Seymour continued, "was to watch their little tongues and become careful of what they say. There is power attached to every word that man speaks, even if it is not directed to the Father in prayer. Man, just like the evil entities, can curse himself or others by speaking bad words into the atmosphere."

We looked across at the meadow and noticed that the farmstead had their chickens out, running around, chasing flies and bugs, catching them and eating them. I enjoyed watching these brightly coloured chickens, some were black with red breasts, and bright red crowns and sharp, beady little eyes.

The flies were tiny, and yet they could find them. They would home in, jump up, and grab the flies – it seemed a great effort for a tiny meal, but those little insects gave nutrients to the chickens' bodies and kept their brains active.

While my gaze lingered on the surroundings, Seymour chatted with the guardians of the mother. They looked like experienced angels, who smiled as they conversed with Seymour.

Seymour turned to face me and said, "These two guardians were like me on one of my first missions, keen to see the enemy destroyed. The enemy doesn't like them and stays well away from them – because they don't hesitate to call for help."

At that moment a bowman arrived and said, "Hi, Seymour, Shiloh, we came back to see if you found anything more. We are going back through portal seven. Do you want to join us?"

We agreed our task was done. This last visit had built on the education I already had. We joined the bowmen through portal number seven and re-entered our realm.

We walked across the heavenly quad. Its shiny sapphire stones glistened and changed colours as heaven's glory animated it. It felt superb to be back.

Seymour taught me that all I needed to do, each time I returned, was to take a deep breath, filling my being with all the good I could, and expelling anything not of heaven on the out-breath.

If only man knew what was waiting for him, I thought, he would change his precarious existence, enhancing his life with everything he could access from us here in heaven, living it fully down there, on his home ground.

I asked Seymour, "Tell me more about how a soul on earth connects with the Father in heaven."

Seymour nodded . "It begins with the realisation that there is an emptiness inside, a void only the Father can fill. When someone notices their need for Him, they can cry out, and the Father hears.

"He designed humankind with an innate longing for a relationship with Him. Though many try to ignore it or fill the gap in unhealthy ways, every soul senses that void deep down."

"A human bridges the divide between realms, between spirit and flesh, through Christ, remember!" Seymour exclaimed. "We know that Jesus is the mediator, the only way a soul can be reconciled to the Father. When someone accepts His sacrifice on the cross, repents, and believes, a door opens within.

"The Holy Spirit rushes in to fill the emptiness with divine light and life. He begins the process of transforming them from the inside out into the Father's likeness."

I nodded. I was beginning to understand it better and better. "It's an intimate relationship."

"Yes! The Father wishes to be involved in every detail of men's lives, sharing all things. As they draw near to Him, He reciprocates. Soon they can sense His presence guiding, comforting, correcting. His voice whispers in their spirit, affirming their identity as His beloved child."

Seymour's face was radiant. "If only they glimpsed how the Father desires their fellowship! No barrier can separate a willing heart open to His Spirit's wooing. In His presence, broken souls find healing. Weary ones, rest. All discover their truest purpose."

I felt stirred. What wondrous intimacy the Father offered people, if only they accepted His invitation into the dance!

At the afternoon class, Ralph gave a lecture on how man prays to the Father.

"When somebody prays," he said, "the prayers go up to heaven and enter the throne room. An angel collects them in a bowl. This angel is adorned in robes that shimmer and are covered in precious stones that sing in delight when the angel moves towards the Father. He hands the prayers to the Father. The Father hears the words from the prayer bowl. As the soul or person prays, the Father hears them , as if He were standing right next to the soul. He also hears to the heart, as it pours out all its words. The Father listens to the prayers that line up with His word, which He has written in the book for the souls to learn about their actual home and actual existence. As they say these promises back to the Father, He orders angels out to go to do His bidding. They are sent out to trap the enemy, to destroy the enemy, and to protect the one who is praying or being prayed for."

I had seen for myself that prayer must never be underestimated. Carol's mother had suffered the same abuse, when she was young, and it took many years for her to overcome it and admit to herself that she had committed self-harm. The curse had been a generational curse that had come down through the bloodline. When the mother received Jesus as the saviour, that bloodline was cut, but , the daughter had already been born. So the end of the curse had only come into its ripeness now, with Carol's healing and her forgiveness

"Class," said Ralph, "you need to understand that man goes through so much. You should have a massive amount of respect and honour for the living souls that you have to look after, because you all know what they might have to face, and you must try everything you can to stop the worst from happening."

Our screens lit up at our consoles and we could all see Carol, still sitting on her bed, again reading a book. There was a glow about her, even though her arms were still bandaged. Her mother came in with a cup of soup on a tray, and beside it was a piece of bread with butter and a cup of tea. This mother was so nurturing, caring, and loving!

We looked on, the mother held no grudge, she was relieved, and thankful to the Father. Mother and daughter prayed together, and we could all hear their prayers.

"Father, thank You for saving my daughter. Thank You for bringing her home to me . Thank You for defending her in her time of need. She could not call out to You, yet You listened to me. Father, you are a true Father. You're a Good God. You have looked after my family. This curse of cutting came to my Carol through my earthly father. You have cleansed our bloodline of these iniquities. I made a huge mistake years ago, but You forgave me and cleansed me, and now You've cleansed my daughter, I just give You All the glory, Lord."

We heard the words go up, we could see them swirling in glowing light of many colours. They had an aroma and we watched as the collecting angels collected them in big golden bowls and walked towards the Father, who was sitting on the throne, and they offered them to the Father.

The words came out of the bowls like smoke comes out of a pit. The bowl billowed with gold and silver and all sorts of precious colours glistening. These swirling colours were never seen on us, they represented the soul's feelings and emotions, which went into the Father and swirled all around Him.

Dancing in delight, the colours mixed into different shades, separated and mixed again, surrounding Him, enveloping Him, whereupon He ordered high-ranking angels to prepare a platoon they should send out. He wrote on a scroll what needed to be done and handed it to one of these angels.

He raised His right arm into the air and said, "Go!"

I looked at Seymour and asked, "Why is He sending more angels to help them?"

"Well, Shiloh, the Father is sending them extra protection. He knows the enemy will try again to get this family, but the family has given the father thanks and has committed themselves to His protection and He won't let them down."

Hordes of angels went out in their ranks, all in orderly style. They moved in perfect unity to do battle. I'm sure I saw big grins on all their faces, because this was what they were made for. One by one, the units went down through the portals and into the earth's realm.

The Father had the angels at His throne capture all the heartfelt words and had them sealed in beautiful bottles. The bottles glistened with the swirling colours. The words of the soul's prayers never rest or sleep, but were taken to the storehouse of prayers, where they were categorised and put onto designated shelves.

Chapter 15

Nature's Sanctuary Defended

After all our exertions, I felt like the action in man's realm was unceasing.

The entities came in many types, as we were many types of angels.

Each entity had its specialist task and dare I say, in an orderly military structure, like ours, but fear and intimidation governed it, rather than sound reason.

These entities existed for the sake of harassing and harming humans, and to bring them pleasure to carry out their orders.

As I pondered this subject, I perceived Seymour eavesdropping on my thoughts. I glanced over to him as he sat on the low wall of portal two. He said: "Yes Shiloh, I am listening, and you caught me, but we have more important issues to investigate."

"The bowmen have once again asked if we want to help. If you want, we can fall over the edge of this low wall and find ourselves in an adventure again."

"Are we going on our own?" I enquired, rather hoping we were not.

"Oh, Shiloh," said a grinning Seymour, "I have a lot of experience, but one thing I have always known is the angel team are as keen to have adventures and they are excellent at there tasks . That is why we are often only observers and can enjoy the spectacle.".

"We've been given the task of caring for a forester," he continued, "who spends a lot of time in wild, natural forest and the forester's wife has asked for help from the Father.

So, they have dispatched our bowman and saboteurs to help him as we stand here dawdling," explained Seymour with an air of cunning pushiness.

An excited screech came from within the portal. My eyes widened with excitement.

"Yes, we had better go," I said, knowing my friend Humba was hovering at the portal's entrance. I walked over to Seymour, stepped up, and over the ledge I went.

Seymour was taken aback, as he had to still gather his belongings and gird his robe, and he peered over the edge . I landed on Humba's back. Looking back, I gestured to indicate he was holding up the whole expedition.

He shook his enormous head so much, his long beard swung up and over his left shoulder, up and over he went. Leerooi was waiting a short distance from Humba. Thud, he landed and stroked his old friend. Humba asked me if I had been having fun.

"Oh," I broke into an excited chatter and told him of all our adventures. Humba did not reply or interrupt as we glided alongside Leerooi and Seymour. The wind was blowing Seymour's hair and his braids flapped in the turbulence.

Humba interrupted my ramblings and said, "Young 'un, his beak pointed ahead we are nearly there, ready, we will descend soon into those trees."

Ahead and as far as I could see was a sea of hues of green that seemed to cover the mountains and hills like a rug, and now and then we observed a clearing. A cottage was snuggled into the clearing, with a small field and fences and a cow or two.

These were not grand buildings, they were covered in a type of grass, smoke wisped out of the chimney, a giveaway that someone was home.

Humba swooped down to the clearing and landed in the field next to the cottage. Seymour scanned the surroundings, as if expecting company.

I noticed a flash of smoky grey to our left by the cottage and I concentrated and was suddenly right next to it – this was a sneaky informer entity.

The informant had long ears with wispy hair and scaly skin, he looked dirty, and his eyes were bulgy and watery and his nose resembled more that of a mouse.

Seymore said,

"Ok Shiloh, come back, let him tell his master we are on our way. That way we are bound to find them all, as they will want to win."

I was back and standing next to my mentor. Humba smiled as he did and said, "You have come a long way, young 'un, hehe," he chuckled.

I looked across from the viewpoint where we stood and the hills rose to be a woodland full of trees, we had just arrived into what we call a wild place.

Well, a forest of many trees, but this forest was not planted by man, it was natural, so the trees were mixed and varied in size and type.

CHAPTER 15

This was for the wildlife, because the whole area was alive, from the tiniest bug to the beasts that roamed these lands.

"I will go up and see what I can from above," said Humba and, as Seymour's ride, Leerooi, was likewise lifting into the air Seymour said, "Ok Humba, Leerooi, you report back soon , we need to know where all the troop is.

We will cover the floor of the forest."

The trees made the area around them dark and clammy as we moved towards them. The shapes, moved amongst the branches – these were entities from the enemy. The entities realised they were not alone.

Some shapes were large, and some small, and some of these smaller shapes changed into unique figures. Some took on the appearance of a man.

the shape-shifting entities would take the form of men to fool men, while others resembled animals. Some formed a combination of man and animal, creating a chimera.

I was not sure how far we had to go before we would have to ask for help from the bowmen and the saboteurs. I needed to find the man who had asked for help.

Herman had sent a message, asking us to do a recon of the area. Herman wanted to know how many and what rank the entities were.

"Leerooi and Humba, what is your report?" asked Seymour.

Leerooi replied, "about thirty, which is a reasonable detachment for a practice attack .half of them are in morording formation and the rest are spread out and relaxed, .I think these entities are on a training or they may be bored."

"I am sure they have a loose perimeter," replied Seymour, "and have no idea we are on to them, very careless of them!" He chuckled.

Humba interjected, "The leader is holding back and giving his orders from his hiding place. He is 100 yards to the left."

As we walked on, the dankness of the forest closed in, and rustling in the bushes became more frequent. The birds of the forest were calling out as we approached and gave us much information as they gave details of numbers and gave us directions.

Nature, as I discovered, is on the side of light, and these forest creatures were friends of ours.

Seymour clipped on his vest and urged me to do the same thing. We were not using our voices to speak, but our minds, as this was less obvious and less detectable. The entities were too busy going about their own tasks to notice our thoughts.

I am confident with the silver vest I had received from the warriors. Underneath my cloak, it gave me a level of protection that always kept me safe from any darts the enemy tried to shoot at me. I also had the sword and the net.

We observed for a while, and the entities ran around and played together, fighting and snarling and biting. They will not have peace. This unsettled state of their being resulted in them always looking to outdo their fellow entities to gain favour from the leader.

In the distance, something moved which looked different to these entities. We could not see the glow or smell the putrid stench that lingered around entities.

It must be a man, as he was more solid, more compact than they, and he was carrying an axe. The forrester would swing the axe easily from one shoulder to the other shoulder and he used a stick in the other hand to help him walk peacefully in the forest.

As he walked, he caught the attention of the group that were hiding in the trees, and excitement arose as they chatted and laughed and jeered and made obscene gestures and shouted instructions to the man.

Who continued to walk in a peaceful, if unguarded fashion.

He was unaware of their presence.

Some climbed down the branches, some stayed on the top, to swing from tree to tree, others were lying in the path, waiting for the unsuspecting man to pass.

Those in the canopy imitated monkeys and other animals in the forest, like squirrels. Others flew, like we do, on their versions of the light boards, although I have to say their boards were not as manoeuvrable as ours.

Yet others walked on the path, directly towards the man, and as they did so, they were bold and confidently chattering amongst themselves, arguing, in fact, how they would influence the man, even while they fought with one another.

As they approached, the man felt uncomfortable. He sensed the difference in his surroundings, and he was looking, watching. Two birds chattered, giving alarm calls. The man is well acquainted with the forest, and all the trees were familiar to him, as was the behaviour of the animals and birds.

The woodsman knew when they were at ease or uncomfortable with their surroundings. They would warn other animals of predators and danger. The animals were in tune with each other. He could read them, and understood he was being monitored by somebody. The local village had many stories of the unseen entities and the mischief they had caused, stories of men losing their minds, coming home confused and disorientated.

The sun was out, flimsy clouds signalled it would be a clear day.

CHAPTER 15

The large forrester took a deep breath and in hailed the grass and wildflowers, as it had rained in the night, and the forest felt revived and alive, but he still, from time to time, felt he was being stalked as if by a hunter and felt uneasy.

He knew the tree he had picked out would be perfect for the job he had in mind.

His thoughts were now more on how to carry the wood back to his house and how he would make the table he had in mind. So, he knew where he was going.

I saw Seymour crouching in the bushes, not too far from the man. Seymour could see a figure approaching the man on the forest path.

One entity, a half–man – with the hairy, four-legged body of a goat, and the torso, with head and arms of a man – stood in front of the oncoming man.

The entity had an enormous bow and a quiver full of arrows hanging from his broad shoulders.

He loaded an arrow and pulled the bowstring back. With a creak, it took the strain, and when he let it go, it sang in the air with a howling and swishing sound. Thump. It entered the man's head.

Smaller entities worked with the arrow; they swarmed around the man's head and used the arrow as a point of contact.

They swore and shouted and cursed the man through the arrow known as doubt.

A haze of grey and yellow vapour filled the air around the man he was not aware of it, but it is a signal of a mugging, a sure sign some entities are attacking a soul and we have become accustomed to these clouds.

The man, Arendt, doubted where he had last seen the tree. This was strange, as every tree was a friend to him, yet he was confused. The entity rolled around laughing, he took such enjoyment in the power he wielded over the unaware man.

Arendt stood in the road, looking ahead, and put his axe down, leaning it against his thigh. He stretched and looked around, but his eyes saw nothing unusual.

Arendt could not see the entities dancing around him and shooting more arrows into his being. The confusion rose and fear came over him. He shrugged and grunted, picked up the heavy axe, and continued on his way.

Where he had last seen the tree was now a mystery. The entities confused him by using the power of the arrows. The arrows affected the man's thinking and made him change his mind often.

He became confused and forgot why he was in the forest. The entities took great pleasure in seeing the power of the arrows at work and continued to fire more into the man. Their laughter filled the forest. It was not pleasant laughter but a mocking laugh.

They had done it. They had broken through the barrier, all because the poor man had succumbed to the fear he had felt. When he thought he was being watched, he opened a door of opportunity, which these entities used. They built on these opportunities till they overpowered and controlled a man.

"Ha-ha," chuckled the chimera. We watched from a distance and counted the arrows that had pierced the man, fifteen of them, all carrying different thoughts, working their way into the man's mind.

As he stumbled around in confusion, he knew he was not in a normal state. Yet he was oblivious to the actual cause.

Seymour motioned with his eyes to the end of the small clearing. There stood a bigger, more prominent entity. He was watching and giving commands to his little soldiers. He was a skilled leader, who had dispatched his team to sabotage the man and inflict harm upon him.

The leader of the horde stood in the shadows and gestured his commands. He expected company, namely, us. But he had not spotted us yet. He edged closer to the chaotic rabble he called his troop.

They were not listening and had got carried away with their attack. He raised his hairy arm, clad in leather braids. The rabble calmed down and waited for another order.

As we edged up closer, A heavy, putrid stench filled the air, like rotten flesh. It was horrible. Even down in this realm, smells like that can be unpleasant.

Seymour grinned and told me to focus on sweet lemons and ants in the roses to keep my attention on positive things.

"Ants in roses?" I looked confused.

"Yea, I love the little guys, they are so clever, they all work together as one, like us – one is always part of many. They sence that we are watching, but he can't see us because our vests are superb at disguising us," continued Seymour.

The powers of our armour cloaked even the smell of our presence. But the chimera was shuffling around. Every few moments, he sniffed the air and scanned the vicinity, and swung around, looking in our direction.

At this stage, we called on the bowmen, as there were too many entities.

CHAPTER 15

We had observed and gone ahead at the request of Herman, who said we were to creep in close and learn as much as we could about the entities, how they operated and who was in charge. Yes, no matter how badly they were organised or disciplined, we had been told under no circumstances to engage.

We needed to pick out who the leaders were.

In the moment that we called upon on the bowmen, the air opened, and there was a blue flash.

They appeared on either side of both of us. Bows were drawn at the ready, and seven arrows flew with a thunder sound.

These immobilisers, known as "thunders," had immense power and could penetrate deep into the target. The leader of the entities fell to the ground, screaming, grunting, and snarling.

I threw my net. It made a sizzling noise as it flew and to sing and I'm sure I heard it say "gotcha" as it bound him to the ground. He could not move, the net held him on the ground and, as he moved, the net drew in on itself and pressed him harder to the ground. As small as it was, the net held. It had a tremendous amount of power.

Bowmen shot and neutralised the entities, and then they commanded the arrows out of the man to return to the owner of the arrows.

The darts flew back into the entities, whatever they had shot into the man, they received it back with an extra power thump from the man. They felt the pain, they felt disheartened, so they became ever more depressed, then angrier and ferocious, and were still fighting amongst themselves, blaming each other for being caught.

The bowmen stood back and watched, and I observed them smile in satisfaction as the fifteen entities were snarling and fighting and biting each other, pushing each other now.

They had been deceived by their own tricks, had been drunk with confidence, which had made them careless – which put them onto another level of sadness and anger, hatred, bitterness, hopelessness, all the things they had meant to fire into the man were now multiplied seven times back into them.

They scuttled off into the forest, now leaderless.

They joined up with the rear gaurd and sculcked away. the job of the bowman was to get the leader as he was causing much harm in the region.

Herman told the sentry angels to come and collect the leader of entities, and he took hold of the leader and bound him with heavy iron fetters and carried him off to a dry place.

The sentry angels were bigger than the bowman and quite different. At first glance, they looked slow and chunky, but it would have been a mistake to imagine they were that. They were jammed with silver plates of armour all around the front.

They did not have free-flowing cloaks, but were clad in several layers of heavy metal sheets and, as they walked, the metal action moved like fabric. It was astonishing, because the whole garment was solid.

If you shot a dart or arrow into one of them, well, all it would do was zing as it deflected off, never penetrating the armour.

The sheets or plates were alive as they shifted from one part of the great angel's body to another, the plates detected the arrows and shifted accordingly.

The sentry angel bent down and picked up the leader. The net fell off on command. My net appeared back in my pouch.

"So, Seymour, I want to know what contrasting thing does this moment in time, yes man's time, have for you?" I asked.

Seymour replied, grinning , "Ah, now I am your pupil!" He played along . "One moment we were chatting to birds and those fluffy four-legged things, yes, you called them squirrels, I enjoyed them chasing each other around the tree trunks. In the next moment, we were in full combat and helping a man." Then he winked said, "Come on, young 'un, we need to get back to class.

We have a lot to report on."

With that, we strolled back to our rendezvous point. The bowmen were still giggling and laughing about the onslaught. Herman bowed his head and said,

"Young 'uns, you did well. You caught a mighty warrior. Well, he wasn't so mighty, he was unprepared," Herman corrected himself. "But you caught him with a well-timed throw of your net. Thank you."

Returning to the main camp, Seymour looked around to find a hole to move through to the portal. The portal had moved helping to stop the build-up of our tracks in and out of the entrance. The entities could not enter the portal, but they could try to lay traps at the entrances.

As we walked through, our boards nudged our thighs, banging gently, almost pleadingly, 'ride us.' Our eagles had already returned to heaven and, well, we did not need to be asked twice. On we got, and off we went. The boards whistled as the light wrapped itself around us and drew us into the next dimension.

CHAPTER 15

We enjoyed going back to classes and meeting our friends. They had sent everybody off on various excursive assignments. Each pair had worked with mentors, and each had had an exciting engagement with the enemy.

"Well, Shiloh, I guess you need a hero's welcome. Not only did you spot the enemy's crew and not get seen, but you shielded the man and called the saboteurs in and threw that net over one of the most powerful entities in the region. Well done,

Seymour, you did well too because you commanded obedience and did not engage. I can't see those reigns on Shiloh anymore," Ralph praised us.

The class laughed. Seymour looked at me and smiled.

Ralph said, "Well, we are pretty impressed by the vests you guys obtained," and with that, the entire class lifted their own cloaks with big smiles, each one revealing a vest of their own.

"What?" gasped Ralph in mock-surprise. "You cannot all have these silver vests!"

Of course, he knew very well that we had all qualified to gain the equipment we needed to be effective as guardians.

Ralph chuckled and said, "Yes, you all may need to get close to enemy entities at times.

You managed to get a close look at the entities and what they were shooting into the poor man, Shiloh, you identified all the arrows and how they influenced the man, causing pain, hopelessness, despair, forgetfulness, all the things the poor man was trying to deal with.

"He has to deal with this kind of attack every single day of his life, and ninety percent of the time he doesn't understand why he has the feelings he does; he rarely knows how to stop them or reverse them. That is where we angels come in –we are to re-enforce man's protection against the deceiver.

"I hope you Angels see that," concluded Ralph, adding, "Shiloh, I congratulate you on using your initiative in throwing your net. Now you can feel confident with it as a weapon as before it proved effective guess this will now be your prime weapon of choice…"

"Yes," I said, "I never would have expected that. I was unsure what would happen when I threw the net for the first time, but this time, I know it would quickly and effortlessly capture him, wrapping around him and securing him to the ground. It was amazing. it was almost as if it had flames and sparks flying around it all the time.

I think the entity was experiencing the reversal of the arrows he had ordered. But I didn't feel empathy for him, as he was a horrible and wicked being, commanding those fifteen entities to cause such havoc in the man's life. He was enjoying every moment –

when an arrow hit, he would duck and squirm with delight as he felt the effects of the arrow affecting the man. It was sad to see."

"Well, class," Ralph said, "as you have seen from your exciting excursions, the enemy is always busy. We need to be attentive, and on guard, and know that our battle groups, like the bowmen, and the saboteurs, are always ready to help. When you are busy with your assignment, you will always need to weigh up the opposition.

Remember, he is deceptive and cowardly, he will try to avoid a frontal assault and will always run when he is outnumbered. He is an inferior creature, but he is also a bully and wants to please his master, even if he causes his own companion's harm. There is one more, probably the most important, thing we need to discuss. Can anyone tell me what that is?" he asked.

"I think I know," I said

"Well, Shiloh, you have the floor."

"I think it would be the prayer that the forester's wife said. She sincerely prayed for her husband's safety when he returned from the forest a day ago, but he seemed disoriented and couldn't remember why he went there. She seemed to know that somehow the entities had influenced him.

It was quite common in that forest, hence the name 'enchanted forest', as it was known to them. Few people travelled into it, and usually they went in small groups. But the forester did not like other people knowing where he obtained his prized wood and he had locations that he visited, so he would always go in alone. His wife knew this made it necessary for her to pray for him."

"Yes, the wife believed in the Father and trusted the promise of help. She had her prayer answered," said Ralph. "Well done again, and now you can go to the dorms and re-tell your triumphant experiences with each other."

Chapter 16

Taking My Place Among the Guardians

I stood amongst my fellow students and mentors, a grin spreading across my face. With a dramatic stretch of my arms towards the sky, I was about to launch into another tale of conquest. But I was was politely interrupted by our wonderful teacher Ralph.

"Well, master Shiloh, we have heard of all your off-grid adventures – hmmm, yes, not all official, I might add," he chuckled, with a twinkle in his eye. "But you've had enough exposure to the mortal realm. Tell us, how did you develop relationships with the souls you observed?

"What do you now think of mankind and his world? What value do you place on the bond between a guardian angel and man after your first-hand experience? And finally, what is your view on the future of humanity?"

I nodded, pondering where to begin. My fellow pupils leaned in, eager to hear my reflections.

"Friends, when I first learned of mankind, we were still discovering our purpose. As you know, the two are intertwined – one cannot exist without the other." Light laughter rippled through the class. They had come to know my dramatic flair.

"When I arrived here and made my grand entrance on my light-board ..." More laughter erupted. Even the birds perched in the nearby trees seemed enthralled.

"I had just left the Father and entered this wonderful company." I smiled as I continued my tale. "I felt at home immediately. Despite knowing nothing, you all showed me what to do. You have my deepest thanks."

Applause thundered through the heavenly forest clearing. Even the smaller creatures peeked out to listen.

"When the Son first told us about the War, I didn't understand His sacrifice for beings so different from us. Why would He help those who didn't even acknowledge Him?" I shook my head, remembering my naivety. "Only when Jesus explained the Father's desire for fellowship with mankind, only then did I understand. We were created to serve, but humans have free will. This was initially beyond my comprehension."

More applause rippled through the class. I went on. "At first I resented and despised mankind's selfishness and lack of desire for the divine. But my views changed here at Angel School, led by our wonderful teacher, Ralph."

Raucous cheers erupted for our esteemed teacher, who bowed his head humbly.

"Ralph showed me that each human has a purpose and destiny. His wisdom inspired me to rise above my own ignorance." I smiled at Ralph gratefully. "But there was another who guided me –an angel wise and kind. He stood by me on every adventure, giving advice and help."

The class cheered, knowing I spoke of my dear mentor, Seymour.

I grinned as I continued, "Yes, Seymour taught me the 'why' behind humanity's struggles. With calm wisdom, he revealed the dark forces that influence mankind – evils we angels scarcely experience."

My voice grew serious. "These forces torment humans' night and day. This is why we guardians are vital. We guide human souls on their journey back to the Father."

My fellow angels sat tall with pride. Our mission was clear to us all.

"Humans face endless obstacles and foes. But we have unity of purpose and love for the Father. We serve not out of fear, but devotion."

Shouts of agreement rose. My comrades brandished their weapons, signalling that they were ever ready for battle.

"Our charges are magnificent in their triumphant return. We simply guide them through the journey."

I paused, letting my words sink in.

" Humanity is the Father's beloved creation. And so, we must be their steadfast guides."

My classmates leapt to their feet, cheering wildly. I smiled, my heart full. What an honour it was to be trained as a guardian angel. A roar emerged from the bushes – it was Carol's guardians, Basra and Kula, applauding loudly. With them, were the bowmen and the saboteurs.

"That's my boy!" shouted Mark. His troupe of fighters joined the ovation, waving spears and swords.

I laughed. "Welcome, friends! Come join us."

Basra and Kula came to sit beside Seymour, giving me a proud nod. My other battle companions followed, including Humba who swooped overhead before perching nearby.

I continued pacing, lost in thought. A gentle reminder from Seymour entered my mind: "We're still here, waiting."

I smiled at my mentor and went on.

"The enemy attacks relentlessly, knowing each soul is cherished. No one is valued above another. So, all feel his wrath." I clenched my fist. "But we have unity, while he only knows fear and division! His corrupted ways differ from our realm of light. And this gives us the advantage."

Shouts of victory resounded. My fellow guardians were with me, we were united by love, unlike our divided foes. I paused, facing my rapt comrades.

"But we do not just watch idly! We actively guide souls toward the light. And mighty warriors like Mark and Herman, and Garrick and Mac, defend from depraved attacks."

Herman rose and flexed his muscles, eliciting laughter.

I went on, "Yes, we guardians have limitations. But wisdom, teamwork, and devotion empower us. With our allies, we outshine the enemy's hatred."

The forest erupted with the sound of applause and victory cries. All my comrades now stood tall, resolve shining in their eyes.

"And with skill from teachers like Ralph, we can outmanoeuvre any attack. Goodness will prevail over evil! Of this I am certain."

Ralph smiled proudly as cheers erupted once more. The birds sang joyously overhead. I placed my fist over my heart, humbled by the honour.

"We may not be mighty warriors, but the love we kindle is the most powerful force of all. It illuminates."

With a final rallying cry, we all raised our swords together in salute. The enemy's days were numbered. Humanity would prevail – with guardians like ourselves lighting the way.

My mentor Seymour rose and approached me, his eyes glistening with pride. He placed a hand on my shoulder.

"You have learned well, young guardian. Now go forth – you are ready."

The class erupted into deafening applause and shouts of joy. My fellow angels swarmed me, slapping my back and shaking my hand.

As cheers rang out, I took my place among the guardians.

Wherever our paths led, our mission was true. Our light would shine through the darkness.

Printed in Great Britain
by Amazon